STARS SO
SWEET

STARS SO
SWEET

Tara Dairman

G. P. PUTNAM'S SONS

G. P. PUTNAM'S SONS
an imprint of Penguin Random House LLC
375 Hudson Street
New York, NY 10014

Library of Congress Cataloging-in-Publication Data
Names: Dairman, Tara, author.
Title: Stars so sweet / Tara Dairman.
Description: New York, NY : G. P. Putnam's Sons, [2016] | Sequel to: Stars of summer.
Summary: "Just as Gladys Gatsby prepares to enter the complicated world of middle
school, her secret gig as the New York Standard's youngest restaurant critic won't
be a secret much longer—and Gladys must enlist the help of her Parisian aunt to be
true to herself, and honest with her friends and family"—Provided by publisher.
Identifiers: LCCN 2015032477 | ISBN 9781101996485 (hardback)
Subjects: | CYAC: Cooking—Fiction. | Journalism—Fiction. | Secrets—Fiction. |
Schools—Fiction. | Restaurants—Fiction. | BISAC: JUVENILE FICTION / Humorous
Stories. | JUVENILE FICTION / Social Issues / Friendship. | JUVENILE
FICTION / Cooking & Food.
Classification: LCC PZ7.D1521127 Sw 2016 | DDC [Fic]—dc23
LC record available at http://lccn.loc.gov/2015032477

Printed in the United States of America.
ISBN 978-1-101-99648-5
3 5 7 9 10 8 6 4 2

Design by Marikka Tamura.
Text set in Bookman Old Style Std.

For my parents, Barbara and Fred,
and my aunt Judy

Chapter 1

LOBSTER LOCKDOWN

GLADYS GATSBY FELT LIKE A LIVE FISH was flopping around in her stomach.

All around her in the school yard stood strangers, talking and laughing—incoming seventh-graders from the four other elementary schools that fed into Dumpsford Township Middle School. They couldn't possibly all know one another already, but somehow it felt like they did, or like everyone there knew at least *one* other person. Gladys didn't have a lot of friends, but she wished now that she had made plans to meet up with one of them this morning before middle-school orientation started.

"Nice stuffed animal," said a snarky voice.

Gladys looked up just in time to see a

girl with a super-short haircut and a green messenger bag melt into the crowd. Who had she been making fun of? Gladys didn't see any kids nearby holding a stuffed animal. Seriously, you'd have to be pretty clueless to bring one here—might as well announce to the world that you were a giant baby.

Still, the drive-by comment had rattled her. Was that the kind of thing she had to look forward to in middle school? Taking a deep breath to compose herself, Gladys stroked the fuzzy strap of her lobster backpack—and froze.

She yanked the backpack off to examine it. Its belly was sunken today, since there wasn't anything inside it other than a lock for her new locker and her restaurant-reviewing notebook and pencil, which she kept with her at all times. But the lobster was made of bright red plush fake fur.

That girl had thought her backpack was a stuffed animal.

In sixth grade, Gladys's lobster backpack had been . . . not cool, exactly, but her classmates had accepted it, probably because they all knew she was a foodie. Sometimes they even came to ask her for cooking advice at recess. But the new kids here wouldn't know that; they wouldn't know she was a professional restaurant critic, either, with several reviews published in the country's biggest newspaper, the *New*

York Standard. To them, she was just a juicy piece of fruit, ripe to be picked on. And if her skin wasn't thick enough, her soft insides could come bursting out at any moment.

"Gladys!"

Gladys spun around and saw Parm Singh racing up to her. *Oh, thank goodness.*

"Parm!" she cried, and when her friend finally reached her, they embraced. "I didn't know if you'd be back from Arizona in time to come today!"

"We just got back last night," Parm said breathlessly. "Though I considered skipping it altogether. Jagmeet went through this same orientation three years ago and said it was pretty useless."

Jagmeet was Parm's brother, and they had spent the entire summer in Arizona together, visiting cousins. Gladys hadn't seen Parm since her own birthday in June, but it seemed that a summer in the desert sunshine still hadn't managed to turn her cynical friend into a bright-eyed optimist.

"So," Parm said, lowering her voice, "what's going on? How was the rest of your time at camp? And your hot dog assignment—did you get your review done for the *Standard*? Did you end up telling your parents about your secret job?"

There was so much to catch Parm up on—but just as Gladys opened her mouth to respond, a bell rang and the doors to the middle school burst open. "I'll tell you everything later," Gladys promised as they got swept up among the kids pushing into the building.

The first stop for orientation was the auditorium, which was just opposite the school's front door. Gladys barely had time to look around the crowded lobby before being herded inside by a man she assumed was a teacher. All of the adults were wearing matching blue T-shirts that had a picture of what looked like a comet on them and the words *Dumpsford Township Middle School: Where everyone's a star!*

"I sure hope the science teachers at least know the difference between a comet and a star," Parm muttered, "or else we're in for a pretty mediocre educational experience."

They took two seats, and soon a woman dressed in the shooting-comet T-shirt walked onto the stage. "Welcome to DTMS, seventh-graders!" she cried. "My name is Dr. Sloane, and I'm going to be the principal for your next two years here." Dr. Sloane went on to explain how the students' schedules would work: eight forty-eight-minute class periods in a day, plus homeroom.

Gladys glanced around the vast auditorium. She spotted another friend, Charissa Bentley, sitting up near the stage with Rolanda Royce and Marti Astin. She also saw a few kids she knew from last year and from camp scattered around. But there were many more new faces, and Gladys wasn't sure how she felt about that. After all, it had taken six years of elementary school just to get used to the old ones.

Once Dr. Sloane finished explaining the absolute necessity of getting a hall pass before going to the bathroom, she cleared her throat. "And finally," she said, "I have an announcement to make about after-school activities. Because of budget cuts, DTMS doesn't have as much funding this year for extracurriculars as we've had in years past. There will still be a variety of clubs and teams offered, but if groups want to take field trips, or purchase new equipment, they'll have to raise the funds to do so on their own."

"Oh, no!" Parm murmured.

Gladys turned to her friend. "What?" The budget cuts didn't sound like such a big deal to her, but she wasn't planning to join any clubs anyway—she figured that her job at the *Standard* was after-school activity enough. Parm, though, looked distraught.

"Every spring, the girls' soccer team goes to the big regional tournament in Pennsylvania," she whispered. "I've been looking forward to it ever since I started Pee Wee Soccer." She frowned. "Then again, I might not even make the team."

"Of course you will!" Gladys didn't know the first thing about soccer, but she did know that Parm practiced harder than anyone else. "And Dr. Sloane didn't say you can't go—she just said you'd have to raise some extra money."

"*All* the money," Parm corrected her. "Do you know how much money it takes to send a team of eighteen girls away for two nights?"

Gladys guessed that it was probably a lot.

Parm and Gladys weren't the only ones discussing this latest announcement; the entire auditorium was buzzing.

Dr. Sloane had to tap the microphone to regain everyone's attention. "There are tryout and sign-up sheets posted on the bulletin board outside the cafeteria for those of you who want to get a jump on your extracurriculars. More importantly, though, you'll be able to pick up your class schedules outside these doors here, as well as your locker assignments. Please use the remaining hour to tour the school and look for your classrooms. You can also test out your lockers and place your new locks on them; teachers will be stationed in every hallway to help you out. Enjoy yourselves, and we'll meet again on the first day of school!"

Out in the lobby, teachers were manning tables with boxes of schedules organized by last name. Gladys went to the *G* station, and Parm to the *S*. When they met up again to compare, Charissa bounded over, her high brown ponytail bobbing behind her.

"Hey, Gladys!" she said brightly. "Oh, hey, Parm."

Parm raised one of her thick black eyebrows in Gladys's direction. While Parm had been away in Arizona, Gladys had spent the summer at Camp Bentley, the day camp owned by Charissa's parents. In that time, she and Charissa had become pretty good friends. But sarcastic Parm and popular Charissa had never really gotten along.

"Hello, Charissa," Parm said coolly. "I trust you had a good summer?"

"Oh, the *best*," Charissa gushed. "I got to swim every day, my team won the color war, and Gladys taught me how to cook West African food *and* let me give her a makeover one night!"

Parm shuddered, though Gladys couldn't tell whether it was over the horrors of makeovers or the horrors of international cooking. Parm was the pickiest eater Gladys knew.

Charissa probably should have then asked Parm how *her* summer had gone, but she didn't. Parm was already too busy comparing her schedule with Gladys's to notice, though.

"I can't believe this!" she grumbled. She held both schedules up to the window, as if illuminating them might change their contents. "How can we not have a single class together? We even both signed up for French!"

This was true, but Gladys had been put into an

eighth-period French class, and Parm had French during third period. They didn't even have the same lunchtime—Parm was in sixth-period lunch, and Gladys had her lunch during fourth.

Wait—*fourth* period? Gladys grabbed her schedule back and looked at the times again. Fourth period started at 10:20 a.m. As far as she was concerned, that was barely brunch time. How was a meal at 10:20 supposed to last her through the next four hours of classes?

Gladys groaned. "This is less than ideal."

"You can say that again," Parm said.

Charissa was peeking over Parm's shoulder now. "Hey, Parm," she said, "our schedules are almost identical."

Parm's voice faltered. "Are they?"

"Yeah," Charissa said, holding out her paper. "We've got art, science, math, gym, lunch, and English together. I'm in third-period social studies and eighth-period French with Gladys, but otherwise, our timetables are exactly the same."

Charissa didn't sound especially thrilled about this, and Parm shot Gladys a look that clearly said *Kill me now.*

"Well," Gladys said quickly, "it's nice that you guys will have at least one familiar face in most of your classes, right?"

She was trying to help her friends see the bright

side—but at the same time, the pit of worry that had entered her stomach in the school yard now felt like it was sprouting into a full-grown tree of anxiety. Two classes with Charissa and none with Parm left a whole lot of classes with zero friends. Her parents would surely advise her to make new ones . . . but Gladys would rather tackle a hundred difficult new recipes than force herself to talk to one new person.

"Come on, let's go find our lockers," Charissa said. "Marti's and Rolanda's are both in the south wing, but mine's in the north. What about you guys?"

Gladys's and Parm's locker assignments were in the north wing, too, so they all set off together in that direction. They reached Gladys's locker first, and she dug into her lobster backpack. In elementary school, they hadn't been allowed to lock up their things, but for middle school, a lock was on the list of required school supplies.

The U-shaped shackle clacked back and forth as Gladys pulled her combination lock out, and its metal felt cold to her touch. She had spent a good half hour the night before practicing her combination to make sure it was branded firmly into her memory; she could think of nothing worse than drawing attention to herself by needing to ask a custodian to break into her locker on the first day of school.

Most kids in the hallway were just slapping their locks onto their empty lockers, not leaving anything inside since they didn't have books or supplies yet. But as Gladys's lock jiggled in her hand, the words *stuffed animal* echoed in her head. Making a snap decision, she shrugged off her lobster backpack and tossed it in. There it slumped at the bottom of her locker, claws drooping. She slammed the door, slid the shackle through the latch, and snapped her lock shut tight.

Chapter 2

A TRUNKFUL OF POTS AND PANS

THE THREE GIRLS SPENT THE NEXT HOUR wandering the middle-school halls together, although Parm and Charissa barely spoke to each other. After finding everyone's lockers, they scoped out their classrooms and places like the gymnasium and cafeteria. Their new school was much bigger than East Dumpsford Elementary, and the longer they wandered, the more Gladys felt like a single chocolate chip drowning in a huge bowl of cookie batter. The only room that wasn't quite as big as its elementary counterpart was the cafeteria, which helped explain why there were so many lunch periods.

"Jagmeet told me the cafeteria food's pretty bad," Parm warned them, "so we'll be safer bringing our own."

Gladys nodded. After a summer of preparing at least twenty lunches a day at camp, it would be a relief to be responsible for just one.

Outside the cafeteria, the girls found the bulletin board with the team and club sign-up sheets. Parm made a beeline to put her name down for soccer tryouts while Gladys scanned over the other options. The Art Club poster had a beautiful lotus flower drawn on it, and the Mathletes one was decorated with equations. Charissa pulled out a purple pen and scrawled her name in loopy cursive on several sheets, including Student Leadership Council, cheerleading, and French Club.

Gladys hadn't planned to join anything, but maybe French Club would be interesting. So many important cooking terms were in French—plus, there was a new reason in her life why learning some extra French might come in handy. She uncapped the pen she found hanging from the bulletin board and added her name.

Parm leaned over. "Oh, French Club? Cool. Well, even if I make the team, I might have time for one more activity—and then at least we'd be in *something* together, right?" She paused briefly when she saw Charissa's signature on the list, but signed up anyway.

Gladys felt the pit in her stomach dissolve a little; at least she would have the first French Club meeting with her two friends to look forward to.

"Shoot—I'm buzzing." Parm pulled a new cell phone with a soccer-ball decal on it out of her backpack. "It's Dad—he's outside. He's on his lunch break, so I shouldn't make him wait. Gladys, give me a call later to catch me up on everything, okay?" She gave Gladys a quick hug. "Uh, bye, Charissa."

Parm turned and sprinted toward the exit, leaving Gladys and Charissa behind. "I'd better go find Rolanda and get going, too," Charissa said with a sigh. "We've already missed two hours of summer ballet for this."

"Right," Gladys said. "See you soon."

Charissa took off in the other direction, and just like that, Gladys was on her own. *Better get used to it,* she thought.

Slowly, she retraced her steps to her locker. The halls were emptier now; just a smattering of kids remained. Gladys spun the numbers of her combination carefully, and relief flooded her body when the lock clicked open on the first try.

Her lobster backpack sat where she'd left it, its beady black eyes staring up at her. "Sorry," she whispered. She pulled it from the rusty-smelling space and slipped it onto her back. Its fuzzy straps felt comfortingly familiar. Not much else felt familiar these days.

As Gladys walked home, she couldn't help but

think back to the moment a few weeks earlier that had changed everything.

She'd been sitting on the sofa after a long day of camp, listening for the sound of her parents' key in the front door. On the dining room table sat two copies of the *New York Standard,* open to Gladys's latest review, which had been published just that day. Gladys was planning on finally coming clean—admitting to her parents that she had a secret job as a restaurant critic and that several of their "family outings" into New York City that summer had been research trips.

She knew that telling them the truth was a risky move; her best friend and neighbor, Sandy Anderson, thought it was an awful idea. But Gladys was tired of lying to her family. And besides, they had all grown over the summer. In the past, her parents had only ever had a taste for microwaved meals and fast food, but with Gladys's encouragement, they'd been learning to eat more adventurously and trust her in the kitchen.

But when the front door of the house opened that evening, it wasn't her mom or dad who walked through. Instead, stepping across the threshold with an enormous rolling suitcase was a woman Gladys hadn't seen since she was seven years old.

"My sweet Gladiola!" the woman cried. "Your auntie has returned at last!"

Gladys could hardly believe it, but as she threw her arms around her aunt, she knew she wasn't dreaming. Aunt Lydia was here, in America—in her house!

They had talked on the phone just a few weeks earlier, and Aunt Lydia had made no mention of an upcoming visit. In fact, Gladys knew that she barely made enough money to cover the rent on her tiny Parisian apartment, let alone a transatlantic flight.

"What are you doing here?" Gladys blurted. "I mean, I'm so happy to see you!"

"Me too," Aunt Lydia said, but already her tone sounded sadder and more subdued than her initial greeting. Gladys waited for her to say more, but she didn't.

Then Gladys noticed that her aunt's outfit wasn't the type of thing she remembered her wearing. Whenever Gladys pictured Aunt Lydia, she was dressed in a flowing silk dress or a bright printed pants set. But today, her aunt wore a ratty pair of sweatpants, an oversized gray T-shirt with the Eiffel Tower on it, and worn-out sneakers. Aunt Lydia even smelled different from how Gladys remembered: less like flowery perfume, and more like . . . cheesy nacho chips? Gladys shuddered. Her aunt was a foodie, just like her; she must have gotten desperately hungry on her flight if she'd actually *eaten* her free airline snacks.

Gladys's parents followed Lydia through the door

and set more luggage down. "Surprise!" her mom cried. "We probably should have called, but we thought that showing up with Aunt Lydia would be way more fun." She beamed, then reached out to give her sister's arm a happy squeeze. Aunt Lydia did her best to smile back, but Gladys could tell she was forcing it.

Not knowing how else to react, Gladys forced herself to be as cheerful as possible, too. "It's a *great* surprise!" she cried. And it was; Gladys's brain felt like a cone in a cotton candy machine, gathering up idea after idea for restaurants she and her aunt could eat at and recipes they could cook together. "How long are you staying?" she asked.

It didn't sound like a weird question when she said it, but the look her parents exchanged behind her aunt's back made Gladys feel like she had just asked something embarrassing.

Aunt Lydia simply sighed. "I think I'd like a bath, if you don't mind, Jen?"

"Of course," Gladys's mom replied. "George, Gladys, would you help bring Lydia's things up to the guest room while I get the tub going?"

Gladys darted forward to grab the trunk her mother had been carrying. It was heavy, and the contents inside clanged when she tried to lift it.

"You can leave that one down here," Aunt Lydia said. "It's just my pots and pans."

Gladys smiled. It was a little strange that her aunt would carry pots across the ocean when she knew Gladys had some, but at least that meant they'd be cooking together, right?

As Gladys's dad headed for the stairs with a suitcase, Aunt Lydia turned to follow. Gladys no longer had anything to carry, but she went along anyway, her mind now replaying happy scenes from her aunt's last visit, when they had traipsed around New York City together eating. It was on that visit that they'd discovered Mr. Eng's Gourmet Grocery, an oasis of high-quality ingredients in the culinary wasteland of East Dumpsford. Aunt Lydia and Mr. Eng were the only adults who knew about Gladys's work for the *Standard.*

That was when Gladys remembered the newspapers on the table. Would telling her parents about her job be such a good idea now? They seemed pretty preoccupied with their new houseguest—and Gladys couldn't help but wonder what that guest would think about her plan. Maybe she should take advantage of her aunt's visit and discuss it with her first. Aunt Lydia might be able to help her come up with an even better way to reveal her secret.

Quietly, Gladys slipped into the dining room. Lifting the corners of the first newspaper as if she were scooping a crepe out of a hot pan, she folded it in half silently, then repeated the process with the second paper. She tucked them under her arm, tiptoed into the living room, and slid them under the sofa.

I will *tell them,* she promised herself, *just as soon as the time is right.*

But over the next two weeks, the timing never seemed right to bring up the issue with Aunt Lydia, much less make a new plan for talking to her parents.

First off, while Lydia took her bath on that first night, Gladys's mother forbade her from asking any questions that might upset her aunt. "She's a bit fragile," her mother explained quietly. "She lost her job at the café and couldn't keep up with her rent, so she's going to stay with us for a while."

So *that* was why Aunt Lydia had brought her pots—and why she seemed so melancholy. Gladys was sure, though, that a few days of cooking and eating together would cheer her right up.

But Aunt Lydia seemed to have lost all interest in good food. Instead of planning outings to Mr. Eng's or into the city, she seemed perfectly content to lie around the house all day in her sweatpants, watching hours of TV and snacking on whatever junk food Gladys's parents brought home. Her trunkful of pots remained unopened. And when Gladys cooked some of Aunt Lydia's favorite foods for her, she hardly seemed to notice. Gladys wanted desperately to help, but she just didn't know what to do or say.

Now, as she let herself into the house after orientation, Gladys heard the familiar strains of the *Purgatory Pantry* theme song blasting from the den. Aunt Lydia was in her now-familiar spot on the couch, no doubt watching another marathon of Planet Food's worst show.

Gladys shouted, *"Bonjour!"* but if her aunt responded, Gladys couldn't hear it over the TV.

"She just needs some more time," her dad had said the night before. "I think your aunt's heart is still in Paris." That was one of the reasons Gladys wanted to learn French—maybe that would make it easier to communicate with her aunt. But for now, she felt as alone at home as she had that day at school. Turning away from the den, she slunk upstairs to her parents' office to log on to the family computer.

She was hoping to catch Sandy online—his grounding sentence for getting kicked out of karate camp had finally ended this week, which meant he was back to using computer screens as much as he could. Just as she expected, his username ("rabbitboy") was lit up on DumpChat.

Gladys was just about to message him when she noticed a new e-mail in her inbox from her editor at the *New York Standard,* Fiona Inglethorpe.

Her heart fluttered. A few weeks had passed since her last review had been published, and Gladys knew that Fiona had been busy restructuring the Dining department since her head restaurant critic, Gilbert Gadfly, had resigned. Maybe, finally, Fiona was getting in touch about her next assignment!

Gladys opened the message.

Dear Gladys,

Once again, I want to thank you for doing such a fantastic job with your hot dog roundup. Even though that was not the review I had intended for you to write, your hard work turned it into a piece that we were very proud to publish.

An effort of this quality deserves a reward—and in any case, I feel that you and I have worked together long enough without meeting face-to-face. So I hope you will accept my invitation to dine as my special guest in the executive dining room on the forty-ninth floor of the *New York Standard* building. Eating here will let us enjoy the culinary creations of the *Standard*'s private chef without compromising your identity (which would unfortunately be the case if we ventured to a real restaurant together, since most of the chefs around town would recognize me, even if they do not know you).

Are you free for lunch this week? Please let me know at your earliest convenience. I look forward to sharing a meal, and also have something important to discuss with you.

Cheers,
Fiona

Gladys stared at the screen, dumbfounded. Her editor wanted to meet? *In person?*

Fuuudge. This was not good news at all.

Chapter 3

FRUIT OF THE DRAGON

BACKYARD. NOW!

Gladys typed the words to Sandy with shaking fingers. This was too sensitive a topic to discuss online. Finally, a single word, *justasec,* popped up in the chat box. Gladys closed the browser, shot down the stairs, and burst into the backyard, heading straight for the gap in the hedge that separated her yard from Sandy's.

"Fiona wants to meet me in person!" she squeaked the moment he arrived. "She's invited me to *lunch*! What do I do??"

Sandy ran a hand through his thick blond hair. "And hello to you, too," he said, grinning.

"Hello," she snapped irritably. "Now can we focus, please? This is a serious situation!"

"Very serious," he agreed. "So serious, in fact, that I don't think I can help you on an empty stomach. My mom needs some things from Mr. Eng's—maybe she'll give me extra money for a snack if I pick them up for her. Wanna come?"

Gladys sighed. "Sure." She was eager to hash things out with Sandy, but she was also never one to turn down a trip to her favorite grocery store.

"Okay," Sandy said. "I'll go get some money from Mom. Meet me out front in two minutes?"

Sandy disappeared back into his house, and Gladys made her way to the front yard. Unfortunately, her own snack funds were pretty low; she'd spent all her allowance on cooking ingredients for French dishes that she'd hoped would tempt Aunt Lydia.

Of course, the *Standard* sent her checks for her published reviews, but she'd gotten into the habit of destroying them straight out of the mailbox so her parents wouldn't learn about her work. They had accidentally stumbled across her first check, and she'd barely been able to explain her way out of that situation. *And anyway,* she constantly reminded herself, *I'm not doing it for the money. I review restaurants so I can try exciting new dishes and see my writing published.*

As they walked to Mr. Eng's, Gladys and Sandy began to brainstorm. Sandy had a great mind for solving these types of problems and had helped Gladys plan her other restaurant-reviewing trips to the city. But this situation had him stumped.

"Maybe the best response is no response," he said, kicking a pebble down the sidewalk.

"*What?*"

"Just ignore the e-mail," he elaborated, "and if she asks you about it later, say you never got it, or that it must've gone to spam. Happens all the time, right?"

"I don't know," Gladys replied. "Fiona's pretty savvy. If I say I never saw it, I think she'll just invite me again."

"But what other choice do you have?" Sandy asked. "It's not like you can actually go have lunch with her."

"Of course not," Gladys said. Telling her parents about her secret job was one thing, but she had no intention of ever revealing her age to Fiona, who thought Gladys was a professional adult restaurant critic. And it wasn't that Gladys had lied to her—she had just never directly mentioned how old she was.

They were approaching the entrance to the Gourmet Grocery now; maybe Sandy would have some better ideas once he had food in his stomach. "What kind of snack are you looking for?" she asked.

"Something unusual," Sandy said. "I need to start thinking about my legacy."

"Your . . . legacy?" Gladys stared at him. Sandy tended to bungle words; maybe he meant something else.

"Yeah, my legacy. You know, the way people will remember me?" He scratched a bug bite on his arm. "School starts next week, and it's my last year at St. Joe's. I've got to do something that'll leave a mark."

So he *was* using the word *legacy* properly—but Gladys still didn't have any idea what he was talking about. "What do you mean?"

"Well," he said, "a lot of the boys in my grade have these . . . reputations, I guess you could call them. Like, 'The Boy Who Gets 100 on Every Math Test' and 'The Boy Who Can Dunk a Basketball.' So I've decided that I want to be known as 'The Boy Who'll Eat Anything.' I was thinking about the meatloaf your parents cooked that time I came over, and it gave me the idea. What could be grosser than that? So if I can just find a few really nasty foods to bring to lunch, my legacy will be in the bag. You know?"

"Um . . . sure. I guess," Gladys murmured, though she couldn't help but think back to the way her classmates (mostly girls) used to make fun of her love of arugula. And that was just a salad green! Now Sandy actually wanted to have a reputation at his school for eating gross foods?

Boys were weird.

Gladys pushed open the door to Mr. Eng's and the bell tinkled overhead, but the sound was immediately swallowed up as they entered the shop. Customers' voices echoed in the small space, and wheels on shopping carts squeaked. In the background, a phone was ringing.

Gladys could hardly believe her eyes or ears. Mr. Eng's Gourmet Grocery was *busy*!

That was a good thing, she knew, but she still couldn't help feeling a tiny pang. Gladys was used to having Mr. Eng all to herself when she came in. She had been planning to ask him for help with Sandy's quest for an unusual snack—but now, as she glanced around, she realized that wouldn't be possible. The line at the checkout counter was four people deep, and Mr. Eng—who had finally picked up the jangling phone—was attempting to take an order and ring someone up at the same time.

"Yes, yes," he was saying into the receiver. "You'd like fifteen Vidalia Visas—I'm sorry, Vidalia *onions* . . ."

Gladys and Sandy would be on their own. "Come on," she said. "Let's check out the produce bins first. Sometimes Mr. Eng has new, exotic fruit on sale."

Just then, a shopper with a full cart bustled by, almost knocking Sandy over. Gladys grabbed his arm and yanked him down the nearest aisle.

"Okay, let's see . . ." she said when they got to the produce section. The bins were, uncharacteristically, in disarray. The one that was normally filled with plums was almost empty, and several cherries from another bin had fallen onto the floor and been crushed by shoes and shopping-cart wheels. It looked like it had been a while since Mr. Eng had had time to restock and clean up.

"Oh, here's something." Gladys reached into a smaller bin with a label that read NEW FROM VIETNAM: DRAGON FRUIT! She pulled out a bright pink fruit accented with pointy green dragon-like scales. "I've seen pictures of this," she said, holding it out to Sandy. "The flesh inside is white, with tons of tiny black seeds. I don't think its flavor is very strong, but—"

"Yeah, but it *looks* cool!" Sandy grabbed the fruit out of her hand. "How long do you think these'll stay fresh?"

That would have been another good question for Mr. Eng, if he was available—or to look up online, if Gladys had a phone (the rule in her house was that she could get one when she was thirteen). Most of the time, she didn't mind not having one, but in a situation like this, Internet access in her hand would be pretty convenient.

"Omigosh. Gladys?"

Gladys looked up from the bin to see Charissa barreling toward her, a pink pair of ballet tights covering her legs. "I didn't know you were coming here today! I asked Mommy if we could stop in to grab a few snacks." She grinned back at her mother, whose arm was weighed down by a full basket. Charissa's super-busy schedule of physical activities meant she was always hungry, and Gladys was glad to see that her mom was finally letting her indulge in some snacks that were more substantial than lettuce.

"Cool. We're here for a snack, too," Sandy said.

Charissa turned, apparently noticing him for the first time. "Oh, hi," she said casually. Sandy was yet another of Gladys's friends with whom Charissa didn't get along particularly well.

"Hey, can you look something up on your phone for us real quick?" Gladys asked. "We need to know how long a dragon fruit will keep at home."

"Sure." A few swipes later, Charissa had an answer. "Three or four days is the max, if it's already ripe," she said, showing Gladys and Sandy her screen.

"Ah, thanks," Gladys said. "Sandy, let's find one that's a little less ripe to be sure it will still be good next week."

"Nah, I'll just stick with this one," Sandy said. "An *overripe* dragon fruit would be even crazier than a dragon fruit! Am I right?"

Charissa's button nose wrinkled like it had just gotten a whiff of that overripe fruit. "That's disgusting."

"Exactly!" Sandy cried. And with that, he grabbed a produce bag from the nearest roller and tossed in the fruit in his hand and a second ripe fruit from the bin. "To try now," he said.

Gladys could only offer Charissa a shrug.

"Ris, come on—you said you were hungry," her mother called.

Charissa gave Gladys a finger wave. "See ya when school starts," she said.

Fifteen minutes later, after gathering the groceries on Mrs. Anderson's list and waiting in the longest-ever checkout line at Mr. Eng's, Gladys and Sandy were back on the street.

Sandy had pulled out his Swiss Army Knife and was now crunching on the melon-like flesh of one of the dragon fruits as they walked home. "Wow, this *is* bland," he observed. "So, why do you think Fiona wants to meet you in person?"

Gladys pictured the e-mail. "She said she has something important to discuss with me. I wonder what that could mean."

"That's not code for 'you're getting fired,' is it?"

Gladys elbowed him. "No! At least, I don't think so. She said the lunch would be a reward for a job well done on my hot dog review." The question was would Fiona stay happy with her work if Gladys refused to meet her in person?

"Okay, well, if you don't want to ignore her, then maybe you can come up with an excuse," Sandy said. "Like, 'I'll be on vacation for the next week' or 'Sorry, but I always walk my dog between the hours of eleven and two, so I can't ever make lunch dates.' Or—"

"Wait," Gladys said. "I think you're onto something.

Only . . ." Her brain was whirring now like the blade in a food processor. "I don't think the excuse should be a dog. I think it should be . . . me!"

Sandy's brow furrowed, and not because his dragon fruit had suddenly turned tart. "I don't get it."

"I'll just tell Fiona that I have a kid!" Gladys explained. "A twelve-year-old daughter who needs me right now because she's stressed about starting middle school." Gladys didn't add that the stressed part was perfectly true.

Sandy cocked his blond head to the side, considering. "That could work," he said. "Because if you can't meet this week, then maybe she'll just have to say the important thing over e-mail, right? And then hopefully she'll forget about the lunch altogether."

"Exactly." Gladys felt pretty good about this excuse. Technically it wasn't quite true, but it wasn't the type of lie that could really hurt anyone.

The moment she got home, she returned to the computer and typed a response to Fiona's e-mail.

Dear Ms. Inglethorpe,

Thank you so much for your kind invitation. Unfortunately, I will have to decline. My daughter is at home during her break between camp and starting middle school. She's been a little stressed about school, so I've promised to

spend all my time with her over the next week. I'm happy
to discuss anything with you over e-mail, though.

Best,
Gladys

She clicked "Send," then sat back in the swivel
chair. Crisis averted—or so she thought.

With astonishing speed, a new e-mail from Fiona
popped up in her inbox.

Oh, good, Gladys—you're online. Hang on a second . . .
I think this will be easier to discuss on the phone. I'll call
shortly.

Gladys stared at the screen, her breath growing
shallower by the second. Fiona was going to call her?

At that moment, the phone rang.

Chapter 4

IN HOT WATER

THE PHONE RANG A SECOND TIME, THEN a third. "Gladys!" Aunt Lydia called up from the den. "Do you want me to pick up?"

"No!" Gladys lunged for the office phone. There was no time to even make a plan.

"Hello?" she said, trying to keep her voice from squeaking.

"Hello, I'm trying to reach Gladys Gatsby. This is Fiona Inglethorpe at the *New York Standard*." Fiona's voice was as crisp as a just-picked apple.

Gladys racked her brain, trying to figure out how to play this situation. Her first instinct was to lower her voice and impersonate an adult. That worked in movies sometimes, but could it work in real life? The last time Gladys had attempted to act was in her third-grade play, but it didn't take a lot of performance skills to play a tree with no lines.

Her lack of confidence got the better of her. "She's not home," she said. "She, uh . . . just stepped out to go to the store. Sorry."

She heard Fiona let out an exasperated sigh. "Drat—I was really hoping to catch her," she said. "And to whom am I speaking, please?"

Gladys could only think of one plausible explanation. "I'm her daughter."

"Yes, of course," Fiona said. "And do you have a name, Gladys's daughter?"

Geez—did they teach you interrogation skills at editing school? Gladys glanced wildly around her mom's desk for inspiration, and her eyes fell on a pile of her own library books that needed to be returned. The book at the top was a creepy one about a girl who stumbles into a parallel world—which was kind of how Gladys felt, spinning stories for her editor right now.

"Coraline," she blurted, and immediately winced. Why couldn't she have said a normal name, like Emma or Sophie? Surely now Fiona would see through her ruse.

But the editor did not appear to be as familiar with children's literature as Gladys was. "Well, Coraline," she said, "can you give me Gladys's cell phone number, please?"

"She doesn't have a cell phone," Gladys said, finally telling the truth.

Fiona sighed again. "Well, then I'd like for you to give her a message. I'm really hoping she can meet me in the city for lunch this week—I have a very important matter to discuss with her. Are you writing this down?"

"Oh, yes," Gladys assured her.

"Good. Then please tell her that I'm making us a reservation for noon tomorrow at the *Standard*'s executive dining room."

"Tomorrow?" Gladys cried. "But she can't! I mean . . . she promised to spend the day with me. This is my last week before middle school starts."

"Yes," Fiona said, "her e-mail mentioned that. So that's why I'll make the reservation for three people. She can bring you along. A lunch in the city—won't that be fun?"

Gladys tried to think of something else to say, but her jaw hung slack. Fiona had finally stumped her.

"So please tell your mom to be at the *Standard* building at noon—I'll meet you both in the lobby. You'll recognize me by my pink suit."

Of course Fiona didn't know that Gladys had already spotted her in person two times before: once at the *Standard* building, and much more recently at the Kids Rock Awards. But Gladys couldn't tell her that, just as she couldn't seem to come up with an excuse to get out of the next day's lunch.

"I'll see you then," Fiona said, and the line went dead.

Double, triple, quadruple fudge. What was Gladys supposed to do now? In a daze, Gladys got to her feet and shuffled out of the room. She wandered downstairs without thinking about where she was going and found herself in the den. Aunt Lydia shifted on the couch, then reached for the remote to turn down the TV's volume. "Who was on the phone?" she asked.

Gladys considered her answer. On one hand, she didn't want to burden Aunt Lydia with more problems when she clearly had plenty of her own. But then again, who else did she have to turn to?

"It was my editor at the *Standard*," she said finally. "I think . . . I think I'm going to lose my job."

The TV snapped off with a click. "Lose your job?" Aunt Lydia cried. "Your reviewing job? Oh, my Gladiola—what's happened?"

Aunt Lydia's face no longer wore the blank expression Gladys had gotten used to; instead, it was full of concern, and the story came bursting out of Gladys like icing from an overfull pastry bag. She told her aunt about the e-mail from Fiona, the clever excuse she and Sandy had come up with to get her out of going to lunch, Fiona's phone call, and the meeting that was now set for tomorrow.

As she listened, Aunt Lydia's spine grew straighter and her eyes brighter. *Maybe the best way to forget about your own troubles is to help somebody else with theirs,* Gladys thought.

"My Glammarylis," Aunt Lydia said when Gladys finished speaking, "why didn't you come straight to me for help when you first got the e-mail?"

"Well . . ." Gladys glanced around the room. The coffee table was covered with crumpled-up fast-food wrappers, and the couch still had an Aunt-Lydia-shaped indentation in it, now sprinkled liberally with nacho crumbs.

Aunt Lydia's eyes followed Gladys's glances, and her lips puckered as if she'd just sucked on a lemon. *"Mon dieu,"* she murmured in French. "It looks like a junk-food hurricane hit this place."

Gladys placed a hand on her aunt's arm. "Don't beat yourself up," she said. "Plenty of people eat things they normally wouldn't when they're worried or sad." She thought back to last Halloween and the moment she'd realized that her red spatula costume actually made her look like a giant misshapen stop sign. She'd stress-eaten an entire plastic pail of candy corn, even though it was full of artificial flavors that she would never use in her own cooking.

"I *have* been feeling sorry for myself," Aunt Lydia

said. "But just because *my* job got sucked down the drain like old spaghetti water doesn't mean that we should sit idly by and let you lose yours!"

Gladys's heart took a tiny leap. She wasn't alone. Aunt Lydia would help her figure out what to do.

"Now," Lydia said, brushing some nacho crumbs aside so Gladys could join her on the couch, "you've convinced your editor that you're not Gladys Gatsby, but her lovely daughter, correct?"

"Yep," Gladys said glumly. "Pretty dumb, huh?"

Aunt Lydia thought for a moment. "Not necessarily. It was a smart move to get yourself—as Coraline—invited to the lunch as well. So all you really need is for someone to go along with you and *pretend* to be your mother. That way, you'll be able to listen in on the whole meeting and get the information you need."

"I guess . . ." Gladys said slowly.

"But who can play the role of the grown-up Gladys Gatsby?"

Gladys was starting to get an idea. "Well, clearly it'd be best to choose someone with some familial resemblance to me, and that person will have to already know about my secret career," she said. "And it would also be ideal if that person has a foodie background herself—that way she could discuss lunch with Fiona without looking like a total ninny." She looked at her aunt expectantly.

Aunt Lydia blinked. "Gladys," she said, "you can't possibly be talking about . . . *moi*?"

Gladys broke out into a grin. "Of course I am!"

"But . . ." Her aunt scanned the room frantically again, then looked down at her pizza-sauce-stained T-shirt. "I'm in no state to be seen in public!" she protested. "And besides, the taint of recent job loss is fresh upon me. I'd only bring bad luck to your meeting. No, my Gladiola—you don't want me."

"Yes, I do," Gladys insisted. "It's got to be you, Aunt Lydia! You're the best fit—the *only* fit. And besides, getting out there and talking to other adults will be good practice for when you start looking for a new job, won't it?"

Aunt Lydia seemed to be out of arguments—which was a good thing, since Gladys was already worried that she was pushing her aunt too hard. If she said no again, Gladys would stop asking. But luckily, she didn't.

"Has anyone ever told you that you're very wise for your age?" Aunt Lydia said. A hint of a smile was playing across her face now. "Well, all right—you've talked me into it. I'll have to make an effort to prepare for my New York debut, though." She gazed around again. "And my first step will be cleaning up this room."

She got to her feet and started gathering up trash from the coffee table. "Then," she said, "we should probably move this conversation to the porch. Lydia

Winslow may be a couch potato, but Gladys Gatsby enjoys the sunshine, *n'est-ce pas*?"

Aunt Lydia led the way out of the room, and Gladys scurried after her. Thinking that she and her aunt had found a solution to her lunch date dilemma was exciting. But the fact that she'd gotten her aunt off the couch—and possibly on a path out of her funk—made Gladys feel even better.

Chapter 5

AUNT LYDIA'S SPECIALTY

THE NEXT MORNING, GLADYS STOOD IN front of her closet, trying to figure out what to wear. She finally decided on the striped sundress her mother had bought for her birthday and added a cardigan just in case the executive dining room at the *Standard* was cold. She then loaded her trusty reviewing notebook and pencils into a small purse. If her lobster backpack was too babyish for middle school, then it definitely wasn't the right accessory for the most important business lunch of her career.

"Well, my Gladiola—how do I look?"

Aunt Lydia stood in Gladys's doorway wrapped from head to toe in sky-blue chiffon. Even her hair was caught up in a turban-like head scarf. It was quite a change from her couch-potato uniform . . .

but still, she looked kind of like a fluffy, pastel mummy.

"Er . . ." Gladys said, "your outfit's a little . . . noticeable, don't you think? I mean, restaurant critics are supposed to blend into the background."

Aunt Lydia frowned. "But I'm not critiquing today, right? Just having a meeting."

"Right," Gladys said, "but still, we want to show Fiona that Gladys takes her job seriously at all times, don't we?"

"I suppose," Aunt Lydia said with a sigh. "All right, why don't you come help me pick something out?"

Gladys followed her aunt into the guest room, where her suitcase was thrown open on the bed. In the month that she'd been there, it seemed she hadn't yet gotten around to unpacking. Gladys began to sift through its contents, but soon discovered that pale blue chiffon was the subtlest material her aunt owned. She cast aside one brightly colored, wildly patterned item after another until her hand was scraping the bottom of the suitcase.

Gladys could hardly believe what she was about to say. "Um—maybe you could borrow an outfit from Mom?"

Aunt Lydia looked as though Gladys had just asked her to eat a bowlful of pig slop. "From Jennifer?" she cried. "My Gladysanthemum, you *must* be joking."

"Remember, my name is Coraline today," Gladys said with a grin, "and no. Mom has a lot of good businessy outfits, and you guys are pretty much the same size."

Aunt Lydia made another horrible face, but she reluctantly followed Gladys across the hall into the bedroom that belonged to her parents, who were both already long gone to work. They'd been excited at Aunt Lydia's sudden interest in getting out of the house and happily okayed the plan for an outing to the city. Gladys opened her mom's closet, and it took her only a minute to find a perfectly respectable beige pantsuit for her aunt.

"Ugh," Aunt Lydia said, holding the suit in front of her as she looked into the full-length mirror. "This color will completely wash me out. I *never* wear beige!"

"Then it'll be the perfect disguise," Gladys said. "Now come on, get dressed—we need to leave for the station."

Fifteen minutes later, they were walking toward the East Dumpsford train station, Aunt Lydia fidgeting and tugging on her beige blazer. Twinges of nervousness were starting to ping at Gladys's stomach now; hopefully her aunt would be used to the borrowed outfit by the time they met Fiona.

As the train carried them into the city, Lydia unbuttoned her blazer, leaned back, and finally told Gladys the story of her inglorious exit from Paris.

"It all began when Monsieur and Madame Devereaux—my bosses at the café—decided to retire," she told Gladys. "They had been wonderful to me for twelve years; I started off as a waitress, but eventually they had me do some of the cooking, too. By the end, customers were regularly requesting my specialties. And they also had me oversee the last renovation, which brought quite a lot of color into the formerly plain café."

Thinking of her aunt's suitcase filled with boldly patterned clothes, Gladys could only imagine.

"But when they sold the business this summer," Aunt Lydia continued, "the new owner had different ideas. She said I could stay on as a waitress, but that all the cooking would be done by her brother, *le chef.* And she also had the entire café repainted the most hideous shade of taupe." Her nose wrinkled. "I can't imagine how she thought anyone would want to eat in a café the color of vomit!"

"Blech," Gladys said.

"I tried to tell her that, but that was my first mistake. Then, when one of the regular customers requested my vichyssoise—that's a chilled potato soup, made with leeks and cream—she made me tell him it was off the menu permanently. And *then,* when that customer never came back, she blamed *me!*"

Gladys could hardly believe this unfair turn of events. "That's terrible!"

Aunt Lydia's eyes were moist, and Gladys could see how much, even now, the injustice stung her. "My job in the café had never paid much," she said, "but I had my routine there, and I was happy. Having my responsibilities taken away from me, though . . . that was painful."

Gladys nodded, and her aunt took a deep, cleansing breath.

"I knew that my new boss was just looking for a reason to fire me, so I decided not to give her that satisfaction. I quit. But finding a new job in Paris turned out to be impossible. So I packed up my things, and here I am."

"I'm so sorry, Aunt Lydia," Gladys murmured. "We'll help you find a new job here. Something even better!"

Aunt Lydia smiled, but underneath she still seemed sad. "I miss Paris every day," she said quietly. "The food, the energy, the people out on the sidewalks. As much as I love being near you, my flower, life in East Dumpsford just cannot compare." She gazed out the train window as the skyscrapers of Midtown came into view. "Though perhaps, if I could find work in New York City . . ." She let the thought hang in the air, unfinished, as the train dove into the tunnel that would take them into Manhattan.

It was an eight-block walk from where their train ride ended at Penn Station to their destination near Times Square, and Gladys and her aunt spent the entire length of it calling each other by their new names so it would feel more natural.

"Would you look at that billboard, my dear *Coraline*?" Aunt Lydia said as they passed a Broadway theater. "*Glossy Girl: The Musical,* now in its sixth smash month!"

"Oh, I've already seen that one, *Mom,*" Gladys replied. "It was atrocious. Zero stars!"

They were still laughing when the *New York Standard* building came into view. Aunt Lydia stopped short.

"Are you ready?" Gladys asked.

Aunt Lydia stared up at the building and nodded, though she suddenly looked a bit pale.

It's probably just Mom's suit, washing her out, Gladys told herself—but still, she gave her aunt's hand a fortifying squeeze.

"Come on," she said. "You're gonna be great."

Then, together, they stepped inside.

Chapter 6

A TEMPTING OFFER

FIONA INGLETHORPE STOOD BY THE security desk in the lobby of the *New York Standard* building, one pink stiletto-clad foot tapping the floor. It was only 11:55, so technically, Gladys Gatsby wasn't late for their meeting. Still, Fiona felt anxious about the proposal she was planning to make to her freelance critic. Would Gladys accept her offer?

There was another reason Fiona was uneasy. Gladys would be bringing her daughter along, and Fiona often felt uncomfortable in the presence of children. Her sister taught elementary school, and a few years back she had invited Fiona to come to Career Day and talk about her job as a food editor. Fiona had asked the kids what their favorite foods were at the beginning of her presentation, and never before had she heard the revolting term *chicken fingers* uttered so many times.

Across the lobby, the glass doors opened, and in walked a middle-aged woman in a beige suit. She was holding hands with a girl of . . . well, Fiona had never been very good at guessing children's ages. She was short, so perhaps eight or nine? How old were kids when they started middle school, anyway?

She waved a pink-nailed hand in the air to beckon the pair over. "Ms. Gatsby?" Fiona asked in a low voice when they drew near. The woman nodded and shook Fiona's offered hand. "Welcome to the *Standard*. I've already had your security badges made up." She passed them two prepared badges that said GUEST.

"And this must be Coraline." Fiona forced as much of a smile as she could onto her face, but acknowledged that it probably came across as more of a grimace.

If the girl was scared, though, she didn't let on. "Pleased to make your acquaintance," she said, and held out her own hand. Cringing slightly at the thought of sandbox germs, Fiona gave the girl's hand a very quick shake, then doused her fingers with hand sanitizer from the pump bottle on the security desk.

"Right this way," she said, motioning her guests toward the elevator. Once they were inside, she pressed a button, and the elevator sucked them all up toward the forty-ninth floor.

The elevator doors opened, and Gladys and her aunt stepped out.

"Here we are!" Fiona said, ushering them around a corner.

For Gladys, the phrase *executive dining room* had inspired images of vaulted ceilings and plush rugs, but this room looked a whole lot like the other rooms here that she had seen with her dad during his tax meetings in the spring. The floor was uncarpeted, the tables and chairs were crafted of plain blond wood, and the room's ceiling was no higher than her middle-school cafeteria's.

There were, however, great tall windows that ran from floor to ceiling all along one wall. *The décor is fairly drab,* Gladys imagined writing, *but the space is brightened considerably by an influx of natural light.* Her hand was almost to her notebook before she remembered she was not actually there to review the dining room. Sheepishly, she retracted her hand from her purse and followed the maître d' to a table in the corner.

"I took the liberty of ordering for us in advance, Gladys," Fiona explained when they had been seated. "I usually go for the salmon, but swordfish steaks are the special today, and they really are magnificent. I hope you don't mind."

Gladys's mouth watered, and she turned to Aunt

Lydia, expecting to see similar excitement on her face. But her aunt still looked quite pale. Thinking back through their silent elevator ride, Gladys realized she hadn't heard her say a word since they'd entered the building. Aunt Lydia had warned her that she might not be ready to return to the world of professional adult interactions. Was she clamming up?

Under the table, Gladys nudged her aunt's leg with her sandal.

"Oh, swordfish—that sounds *m-magnifique*," Aunt Lydia stammered. "*Merci.* I mean—thank you."

Uh-oh, Gladys thought. They had specifically agreed that Aunt Lydia should avoid peppering her speech with French words, since that might trigger unnecessary questions. Lydia must have been even more nervous than Gladys had realized.

They had also agreed that Gladys should talk as little as possible—but someone had to fill the awkward silence that was now enveloping their table. "My mom used to live in France!" she declared. "She worked as a cook there."

"Oh, really?" Fiona said, leaning in closer. "I don't remember reading about that in your application letter. When was this?"

Fudge. "Oh, when she was younger," Gladys said quickly.

"Where in France did you live?" Fiona asked. "Was it Paris?"

Paris seemed to be the magic word that finally released Aunt Lydia from her silent spell. "Oh—yes," she said. "I lived in the eighteenth arrondissement. Do you know Paris well?"

"I do!" Fiona said, and there followed a pleasant conversation about Parisian neighborhoods and eateries. It turned out that Fiona and Aunt Lydia had the same favorite *creperie* in the Latin Quarter, and they both spent several minutes lamenting their lack of ability to reproduce such delicately delicious pancakes at home.

Gladys actually had a pretty good crepe-making technique, but she held her tongue; by no means was she supposed to reveal her own prowess in the kitchen. Instead, she sipped the ice water the server had brought. Her stomach was starting to rumble with all the food talk—she had been too nervous to eat much breakfast that morning. So when the server returned with three covered dishes on a tray, she could hardly wait to dig in.

That is, until the waiter removed the dish covers. Unlike the other two, Gladys's plate was piled with . . .

"Chicken fingers!" Fiona announced triumphantly. "Just for you, Coraline. We don't get many children in the *Standard* dining room, so I made sure to put in a special order."

Gladys gazed sadly at her aunt's succulent-looking

swordfish, grilled to perfection and dressed with what looked and smelled like a coulis of tomato and saffron. The only sauce on *her* plate was ketchup in a little metal cup.

She would normally have railed against this underestimation of young people's palates . . . but her mission today was not to draw any extra attention to herself. So "Coraline" merely said "Thank you" in a small voice and dunked one of the fingers into the ketchup. The taste actually wasn't terrible—it turned out that chef-made chicken fingers were definitely better than whatever processed stuff they churned out at Fred's Fried Fowl. But it was still hard not to be bitter as she watched her aunt slice into her hearty swordfish and raise bite after delicious bite to her lips.

"Now, Gladys," Fiona said, "lovely as it is to meet you, this *is* a business lunch. And the first order of business I'd like to discuss is your compensation. It's come to my attention that none of the checks we've sent you for your reviewing work have been cashed."

Gladys nearly choked on her chicken finger. Her practice of destroying the *Standard*'s checks had finally caught up with her.

"Oh, *mon dieu*," Aunt Lydia murmured. She shot a sidelong glance at Gladys that seemed to ask what on earth she had been doing with her checks, but Gladys could do nothing but cringe.

At least Aunt Lydia was able to think fast. "I'm so sorry," she continued. "I've been a bit distracted this summer and have been meaning to make a bank run. I'll deposit the checks right away."

"Good," Fiona said. "Then we can move on to the real reason I asked you to come have lunch with me."

Gladys leaned forward slightly, and Aunt Lydia did the same.

"As you know, Gilbert Gadfly is no longer with the paper," Fiona said. "Which means that we're looking to take on another permanent restaurant critic. I know you've only been freelancing for us for a short time, but based on your excellent work so far—especially with that unexpected hot dog review—I think you would be a strong candidate for the position."

Under the table, Aunt Lydia gripped Gladys's hand. "Are you offering Gladys—that is, *me*—a full-time job?" she asked.

"I am," Fiona said matter-of-factly.

It was a good thing Gladys wasn't holding any silverware in her other hand, or it would have clattered down loudly onto her plate. As it was, she had to remind herself to keep breathing. She squeezed her aunt's hand back.

"I . . . um . . . well, I'm very flattered," Aunt Lydia said carefully. "I really don't know what to say."

And Gladys knew that her aunt was telling the

truth. In their discussion the night before, they had speculated about what Fiona might want to discuss, and it had occurred to Gladys that there might be a job opening now that Mr. Gadfly was gone. But she hadn't thought that Fiona would consider *her*—she'd assumed the editor would want to hire someone with more experience for the position. Clearly, she had been wrong.

"Well, are you interested?" Fiona asked.

Aunt Lydia shot Gladys another questioning glance, probably trying to get a hint for how she should reply. But Gladys, who was still processing the offer, could only give her aunt the tiniest of shrugs.

"Well, of course I'm *interested*," Aunt Lydia said, "but unfortunately, that's not the only issue. After all, I do have my daughter here to think about. She's about to start middle school, which means that her schedule will be much more demanding than it has been in the past."

Gladys nodded vigorously. Her aunt raised a good point—there was no way she'd be able to juggle all of her middle-school classes and full-time work, especially considering that the work would probably mean coming into the city every day. It was an extremely flattering offer, but Aunt Lydia would have to say no on their behalf.

No wasn't the word that came out of Lydia's mouth,

though. "However . . ." she continued, "maybe we could work something out. If Coraline could accompany me to the office sometimes, and on reviewing outings . . ."

"Wait—what?" Gladys couldn't help her outburst. What on earth was her aunt talking about?

"I'm just thinking out loud, my Gla—er, my Cornflower," Aunt Lydia said, quickly correcting herself. "Nothing's been decided yet."

"Indeed," said Fiona, who didn't seem to have picked up on Lydia's flub. She pushed her empty plate away and folded her hands on the table. "And actually, you have a bit of time to make your decision. Despite the major drop in my department's payroll with Mr. Gadfly's departure, the *Standard*'s business department won't approve a new hire until the new year. And even then, they say that I can only bring on a new person if I cut our freelancer budget. As our subscriber base ages, our margins are shrinking," she explained, "and all the departments are being asked to make do with less."

Gladys froze, a fresh chicken finger halfway to her mouth. Budget cuts—just like the ones that were messing with Parm's soccer trip at school. But what did this mean for Gladys's freelance work?

"Excuse me," she blurted, "but are you saying you won't be able to keep Mom on as a part-time reviewer if she doesn't take the permanent job?"

Fiona blinked at Gladys in surprise, but when she

answered, she addressed Aunt Lydia. "Unfortunately, yes," she said, "which is all the more reason for you to accept my offer. You wouldn't be starting until January, but I would like to know your decision by the end of October at the very latest. That way, if you decide not to take the position, I'll still have time to hire someone else."

"Of course," Aunt Lydia said. "But how will the department function down one reviewer for the next few months?"

"An excellent question," Fiona said, "and one I've brought up with our business department many times. However, it seems unlikely that they'll budge. In the meantime, our second-string full-time critic, Natalia Bernstein, will be taking on extra reviews to help fill in, as will our freelancers. Which brings me to our final order of business: your new assignment."

Gladys sat up a little straighter. This was one part of the meeting that she *had* anticipated. Where would Fiona send her next?

Fiona reached into her suit pocket and passed an envelope across the table. "You really seemed to enjoy the Chilean hot dog, the completo Italiano, that you discussed in your last review," she said, "and it got me thinking about how much even we foodies tend to lump the cuisines of Latin America together, when actually they are quite distinct. So I'd like to see a series of three reviews comparing and contrasting the

Salvadoran, Cuban, and Peruvian restaurants whose names you'll find in this envelope. How does that sound?"

"That sounds great!" Gladys cried—but this time, it was her turn to get a kick under the table from Aunt Lydia. *Oh, right—Fiona wasn't talking to her.*

"What I think Coraline means," Aunt Lydia said through tight lips, "is that sounds like a great fit for *me.* She knows how much I enjoy those cuisines."

"Oh, good," Fiona said. "I'd like to start publishing these pieces within a month, starting on September twenty-fifth."

"No problem," Aunt Lydia said. "I can't wait to get started." She tucked the envelope into Gladys's purse. Gladys smiled.

Lydia and Fiona then spent the next few minutes discussing more details about the job offer. It seemed that a full-time critic reviewed at least one restaurant every week rather than one a month, which was Gladys's usual pace. And as Gladys had suspected, she would also be given an office in the *Standard* building, where she would be expected to write her reviews and attend brainstorming meetings with the rest of the department. The offered salary sounded like a lot of money, but then again, she was used to writing her reviews for free. By the time Fiona signed their lunch bill, Gladys's brain felt like a hot broth in which endless number- and dollar-sign-shaped noodles were bobbing around.

Fiona stood up from the table, and Aunt Lydia and Gladys quickly followed. Gladys was a little bummed that the executive lunch hadn't included a dessert—but then again, she probably would have been served a boring dish of chocolate ice cream while the adults got something more interesting, like pomelo bread pudding or rosewater flan.

On their way out, Fiona shook Aunt Lydia's hand again, then reached out and gave Gladys an awkward pat on the head. "Well, good luck with middle school, Coraline," she said, "and do try to persuade your mom to come work for us, okay?"

"Um, I'll do my best," Gladys said.

As they rode down in the elevator, Gladys pinched herself. The pinch hurt, which meant that the job offer hadn't been a dream. But if it *had* been a dream, would it have been a good one or a nightmare?

Chapter 7

PIE IN THE SKY

ON THE TRAIN BACK TO EAST DUMPSFORD, Gladys opened the envelope from Fiona. The restaurants listed were all in Queens. She glanced across at her aunt, who was applying dark lipstick now that their lunch was over.

Lydia had been quiet since they'd left the *Standard,* and Gladys appreciated that she hadn't pressed her to talk about everything that had happened. Gladys needed time to think about Fiona's proposal and her new assignment. She couldn't accept the full-time position at the *New York Standard*—but she also didn't want to lose her freelance job.

Finally, Gladys cleared her throat. "Thanks so much, Aunt Lydia, for everything," she said. "You were terrific today."

Her aunt shook her head as she

snapped her lipstick case shut. "I can't believe how nervous I was. I would have failed utterly without all of your quick thinking. Thank *you*."

Gladys smiled. "We make a good team."

"Well, I meant what I said in there," Aunt Lydia said, her voice starting to sound more enthusiastic. "I bet we could find a way to do this full-time job together. We could both visit the restaurants; I could be the one to go into the office, and you could help me write the reviews. You were talking about my getting a job here in New York," she added. "Well, this could be it!"

Gladys paused to consider. Could it really work? This was certainly the most excited she had seen her aunt get about anything since arriving on the Gatsbys' doorstep. But still, critiquing restaurants had always been Gladys's job, and Gladys's alone. She wasn't sure she was ready to share.

"I didn't know you were interested in becoming a restaurant critic," she said.

"Well, my pie-in-the-sky dream would be owning my own café," Aunt Lydia replied, "but you need savings to start your own business, and if I had any savings . . . well, I wouldn't be living in your parents' guest room now, would I?" A sad little laugh escaped her crimson lips. "So maybe 'restaurant critic' isn't a job I thought I'd ever be doing . . . but I think I'd be happy as long as I was working with food."

Gladys thought hard. She needed a way to get to those three restaurants over the next few weeks, and her aunt certainly had time to take her. They could partner up for these freelance assignments, and see how it worked out . . .

"I'll think about it," Gladys said. "In the meantime, though, how would you feel about an outing to eat Salvadoran food in Queens?"

As they walked home from the train station, Gladys and Aunt Lydia passed Mr. Eng's.

"I remember this place!" her aunt exclaimed. "It has that wonderful refrigerator filled with cheeses from around the world. Just thinking about it makes my mouth water."

"Let's stop in," Gladys suggested. She wanted to scope out the Latin ingredients section, anyway—maybe they could try out some Salvadoran recipes together before visiting that first restaurant.

There weren't so many people in the shop today—maybe five or six—but Gladys could tell immediately that Mr. Eng was still overwhelmed. The light in the cheese refrigerator was out, the shelf of canned tomato products was a mess, and a half-open cardboard box of cinnamon bottles by the spice wall suggested that Mr. Eng had been interrupted while restocking.

Suddenly, an idea came to Gladys. "Mr. Eng!" she cried when she spotted him moving down an aisle.

"Oh, hello, Gladys!" He hurried forward. "How can I help you?"

"This is my aunt Lydia," she said, indicating her aunt. "You met her once before, a long time ago."

"Nice to see you both," Mr. Eng said, though his eyes were already cutting over to the disarrayed shelf; it was clear he didn't have much time for pleasantries.

"Aunt Lydia is new in town," Gladys continued. "She has a lot of experience in the food industry, and she's looking for a paying job. And *you* look like you could use some help around the store." Gladys glanced between their surprised faces. "Sooo . . . what do you think? Maybe she could be your assistant?"

"Gladys!" Aunt Lydia cried. Her cheeks were turning red enough to match her lipstick. "How could you put this nice man on the spot like that? I didn't put her up to this, Mr. Eng, I swear."

"Well, she's an observant one, our Gladys," Mr. Eng said with a chuckle. "I *could* use some help around here." He removed his spectacles to rub his weary eyes, and when he put them back on, he gave Lydia a piercing look. "Let's see now," he said. "Can you tell me which kind of fruit paste matches best with manchego cheese?"

Aunt Lydia thought for a moment. "Quince paste," she said finally.

Mr. Eng nodded, then glanced over at his wall of spices. "What would you sell someone who wanted to make garam masala powder at home?"

This time, Aunt Lydia didn't miss a beat. "Cumin, coriander, cardamom, peppercorns, and cinnamon," she said. "Plus maybe some nutmeg and cloves—or hot pepper if they like it spicy."

Mr. Eng nodded again, looking more impressed this time. "And what kind of potato would you sell someone looking to make a traditional French potato-and-leek soup?"

This time, instead of answering, Aunt Lydia smiled as she strolled over to a vegetable bin, plucked out two large brown-skinned baking potatoes, and held them up. "Vichyssoise is my specialty," she said proudly.

"You're hired!" Mr. Eng beamed. "You can begin on Monday at eight a.m.; we'll be doing inventory."

"Well, thank you!" Aunt Lydia said, sounding a bit shocked.

"Don't thank me," Mr. Eng replied. "Thank this young lady here. Somehow, she always manages to bring me the help I need."

Now Gladys felt herself blush.

"Go ahead and keep those potatoes," Mr. Eng told her, "and grab any other ingredients you need to make your soup—on the house."

Ten minutes later, Gladys and Aunt Lydia were on their way home with bags filled with beans and fine masa corn flour for Salvadoran cooking, plus pota-toes, cream, and leeks for Aunt Lydia's soup.

"Two job offers in one day!" Aunt Lydia crowed. "I'll finally have an income again—I can hardly believe it!"

"See?" Gladys said. "Good things happen when you leave the house."

Aunt Lydia beamed at her. "Thank you, my Gladiola," she murmured. "You're my sweet star."

That evening, the Gatsbys celebrated Aunt Lydia's new position at the Gourmet Grocery with deep, creamy bowls of homemade vichyssoise.

That Sunday—the night before the first day of school—Gladys met Sandy next door in the Rabbit Room. Sandy let his rabbits out to hop freely around his obstacle course of toys, and chubby brown Dennis Hopper made his usual slow progress toward his favorite resting spot on the beanbag chair. But feisty little black-and-white Edward Hopper shot straight across the room toward Sandy's computer.

"Oh, no you don't!" Sandy cried, bounding after him. He scooped up the kicking rabbit just before he reached his destination. "He's been in a real wire-nibbling phase recently," he explained as he carried Edward back over toward the toy area, "and I *don't* want him chewing through any important cables. Hey, Gladys, could you grab that kale? It might distract him for a little while."

Gladys took a fan-shaped leaf of the dark green vegetable off a plate Mrs. Anderson had left with them.

In seconds, Edward was happily munching kale out of her hand, and Dennis soon hopped over, enticed, as always, by the promise of food. Mrs. Anderson's garden had produced an abundant crop this year, so there was plenty on hand for rabbit snacks.

"So," Sandy said, dropping to the floor beside her. "Did you see my dragon fruit up in the kitchen?"

"Yeah, your mom showed me," Gladys said. She'd been relieved, actually—there were no signs of mold. It certainly didn't look as appetizing as it had a few days ago, but Gladys didn't think that Sandy would be in danger of food poisoning or anything when he ate it. "Looks like you're all set for tomorrow."

"Yeah, I'm excited," Sandy said. "How about you? Middle school should be fun, huh?"

"Uh, sure," Gladys said, though all she could really think about was how many new people there would be, and how few friends shared her classes. She ran her fingers over Dennis Hopper's soft brown head, which calmed her a little—and thankfully, Sandy's lightning-quick brain was already on to a new subject.

"Okay, so you have to tell me all about your date with you-know-who."

"My . . . w-what?" The panic surged back, even stronger this time. It had been weeks since Gladys's night out with famous tween author Hamilton Herbertson in New York City at the Kids Rock Awards and then a South African restaurant. Sandy had never asked her for any details about the outing—Gladys refused to think of it as a "date." But that was just as well, because she definitely didn't want to tell him about the awkward kiss that had ended the evening. Plus, Gladys hadn't even heard from Hamilton since camp had ended.

Why was Sandy suddenly bringing it up, out of the blue?

"Yeah," he continued. "You know, your lunch date? With . . ." He glanced at the Rabbit Room door to make sure it was shut, then lowered his voice anyway. *"Fiona?"*

"Oh." Gladys breathed an enormous sigh of relief; Sandy wasn't talking about Hamilton at all. "Right. There's a *lot* to tell!"

As Edward and Dennis munched their kale leaf down to its ribs, Gladys filled Sandy in about Aunt Lydia's spotty acting, the mention of her uncashed checks, the chicken fingers, and the kicker: her job offer to work full-time for the *New York Standard.*

"And if I don't take the offer, I won't be able to work there as a freelancer anymore," she said. "So it's basically make-or-break time for me. I have until the end of October to decide."

Sandy let out a low whistle. "Whoa, Gatsby. That's a lot to take in."

"It is," Gladys said, "but Aunt Lydia and I have an idea. Maybe we could keep working as a team, with her going into the office and me writing the actual reviews. We're gonna work together on my next three freelance assignments and see how that goes."

Sandy shook his head.

"What? You don't think that's a good plan?" Gladys asked.

He sighed. "I just think there could be a lot of logisteral problems, that's all."

"Um . . . *logistical*?" Gladys asked.

"Yeah, that," Sandy replied. "I mean, you said Fiona was already asking questions about your freelance checks—it's basically a miracle that you've gotten away with not cashing them. But if they put 'Gladys Gatsby' on the full-time payroll, then surely *someone* will figure out that the person they're paying is only twelve!"

Gladys frowned; she hadn't exactly thought that detail through. "Well, maybe they could make the checks out to Aunt Lydia," she proposed. "We could tell them that 'Gladys Gatsby' has been a pen name all along, and that she doesn't really exist."

Sandy stretched up to grab a fresh piece of kale off the table; to Gladys's annoyance, the rabbits immediately abandoned her and hopped over to him.

"Your aunt's name on your checks and your published reviews," he said as Edward and Dennis took their first crunchy bites from his leaf. "Is that really what you want?"

"I don't know," Gladys admitted quietly. A couple of days ago, she had felt excited by the prospect of teaming up to take on this full-time job, but Sandy's arguments were making her feel a lot less sure. Letting Aunt Lydia be the "face" of Gladys Gatsby was one thing, but was she really ready to let her aunt's byline replace hers, too?

"And there's another problem," Sandy continued. "How would you manage all those extra reviews on top of the homework you're bound to get in middle school?"

Gladys thought of Hamilton Herbertson once again. He managed his demanding career as a best-selling author because he was homeschooled. Could that work for her, too? The prospect of never setting foot back in that huge middle-school building actually sounded kind of nice. "There's always homeschooling," she said. "I know someone else who does it."

Sandy still didn't seem convinced. "Are your parents gonna go for that? Especially if they don't even know the reason you want to do it?"

"Well, I'd have to tell them about my job," Gladys said. "I mean, I almost told them a few weeks ago, but then my aunt showed up and sort of messed up my plan."

A loud crunch sounded as Dennis bit into the thick stem of the kale leaf, and at the same time, a groan of exasperation escaped Sandy's lips. "Gatsby, you *can't* tell them! I mean, Mr. and Mrs. Microwave? They are *not* gonna get it."

"They've been a lot better," she said quietly. "You know, about food and cooking and stuff."

"Letting you cook dinner a couple of times a week is *not* the same as giving you permission to quit school to become a restaurant critic," he said. "Sorry."

Why did Sandy have to be so negative? With a bit more force than was probably necessary, Gladys swiped the last kale leaf off the plate and waved it at the Hoppers, reclaiming their loyalty.

"Well, anyway, nothing's decided yet. And in the meantime, I get to review three Latin American restaurants." She told him about the different cuisines she would be covering for her next assignments.

This, at least, was something they could agree was pretty cool. "Excellent," Sandy said. "Can I come on one of your research trips? Which one do you think will have the best desserts? I'll come to that one."

Gladys laughed. "Well, chocolate does originally come from Central America . . ."

They parted a short while later, Sandy wishing Gladys a good start to middle school, and Gladys wishing Sandy luck in his quest to become the gross-foods

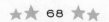

king of his sixth-grade class. "Thanks," Sandy said as he let Gladys onto his front porch. "A slightly mushy dragon fruit in my lunch box should definitely get me off to a good start!"

As she crossed the lawn, Gladys could only wish she had a fraction of his confidence about her own first day.

Chapter 8

A SOUR NOTE

THE NEXT MORNING, THE MIDDLE-SCHOOL hallways were loud and crowded, just as Gladys had expected. Keeping her head down, she wove in and out of groups of students, grateful that she had carefully charted a course to homeroom at orientation.

The thick canvas straps of the plain blue backpack she had found at the back of the hall closet felt strange on her shoulders, and she was happy to shrug it off onto one of the desks when she reached her classroom. Right now, it only contained a few blank notebooks, a pencil case, and a carefully sealed container of leftover vichyssoise for lunch. But Gladys knew it would only get heavier as she received textbooks from each class throughout the day.

The morning bell rang, and Gladys glanced around the room. There were a couple of kids she recognized—Peter Yang and Marina Trillesby—but a lot more she didn't. The homeroom teacher, a man in a bow tie named Mr. Swanberg, took attendance, then made an announcement.

"Since it's your first day of school, there will be a special assembly today," he said. "Instead of having your regular eighth-period class, you're all to proceed to the auditorium."

Gladys stifled a groan. Eighth period was when she had French, the *one* class she was truly looking forward to. Why couldn't the assembly have been scheduled during gym?

Peter Yang waved a hand in the air. "What's the assembly about?" he asked.

"I believe you will be hearing from a special guest speaker." The teacher adjusted his bow tie and glanced over at the clock. "There are three minutes left in the homeroom period, so I'll let you go a little early in case you need to deposit anything in your lockers."

The noise level in the classroom rose as kids made their way to the door. Marina was already chatting with a girl Gladys didn't know, and Peter was getting grunted compliments on his *Keep Calm and Carry a Lightsaber* T-shirt.

How is it so easy for some kids to make new friends? Gladys wondered. Most days, she could barely believe there were four people in the world who liked hanging out with her. But then again, Sandy didn't go to her school, she hadn't heard from Hamilton in weeks, she had no classes with Parm, and Charissa had plenty of other admirers. Plus, each grade at DTMS had five times as many kids as her sixth-grade class had in elementary school. Now even four friends didn't sound like a very strong number.

The rest of the morning passed in an adrenaline-fueled blur; in every class, the teachers introduced themselves, passed out textbooks, and talked about what they would be teaching over the coming year.

Some of the teachers assigned seats, and some let students pick their own. In third-period social studies, the first class she had with Charissa, their teacher, Ms. Webster, let them choose their own seats, so the girls sat side by side. Something about Charissa seemed different today, but Gladys couldn't put her finger on it. Still, she felt relieved to have her friend nearby.

"What have you got next?" Charissa asked as they packed their bags at the end of the period.

Gladys double-checked her schedule. "Oh, right," she said. "I have lunch."

"Fourth-period lunch?" Charissa screeched. "How is that a thing? It's not even eleven o'clock yet!"

"I know," Gladys said. "I guess it's the only time they could fit some of us in."

Charissa scowled. "Well, that's ridiculous. I'm going

to take this up with the Student Leadership Council, for sure—our first meeting is tomorrow. You should come, too!"

"Oh, uh . . ." Gladys knew that joining clubs might be her best bet for building her roster of friends, but Student Leadership *really* didn't sound like the right fit for her. She knew she was much better at lurking behind the scenes—observing and scribbling in her journal—than she would be at leading the masses that thronged this school's halls. "That's okay," she said, "but I think you'll be great at it."

"Of course I will." Charissa tossed her chestnut hair over her shoulder, and Gladys finally realized what was different about her friend today: Her locks hung long and loose, free of their signature high ponytail.

"Hey!" Gladys cried. "Your hair!"

"You like?" Charissa tossed it again and posed with a hand on her hip. "I decided to try something new. I mean, we're in middle school now. Stuff's changing."

"Yeah," Gladys murmured. "You can say that again."

She and Charissa parted ways at the door, and Gladys stopped at her locker before heading to the cafeteria. It was already bustling, and she recognized a few kids at different tables, but nobody waved her over to sit with them. *That's okay,* Gladys told herself. *I could use a little downtime.* She even sort of believed it—after all, she hadn't had time to write in her re-viewing journal in ages.

She found an empty seat at a table in the corner and took out her soup and the small blue notebook she had picked up with her school supplies. Who needed lunch friends when she had blank pages to fill? Her aunt would surely appreciate a review of the vichyssoise, even though today it would be served closer to room temperature than cold. Gladys began to eat and write.

With time, the potato soup has thickened and its flavors mellowed. Now, each spoonful has a delightfully velvety texture and subtle taste that truly allows the simple ingredients—potatoes and leeks, but also butter, good chicken stock, and cream—to shine.

If only the atmosphere in which it was served was as elegant as the soup itself! Unfortunately, the DTMS cafeteria has walls the color of an avocado—an old avocado that's starting to brown. It makes a rather less-than-appetizing atmosphere for lunch, and added to the fact that it's way too early in the day to eat lunch, this critic really does have to question whether the administration of this school has its diners' best interests at heart.

"What are you writing?"

Gladys whirled around to see a girl with sharp black eyes and very short hair peeking over her shoulder.

Quickly, Gladys closed her notebook. "Nothing."

"That's not true—I saw you writing. I even read some of it. A critique of the school's lunch-scheduling priorities, huh? That could make a really good op-ed."

Something about the girl's voice rang a bell, but the bell played a sour note. Who was she?

"I'm Elaine de la Vega," the girl said, as if she had read Gladys's mind. Without asking, she slid into the adjacent empty seat. "Eighth-grader. And editor in chief of the *DTMS Telegraph*."

"The what?" Gladys knew she wasn't being very polite, but she hadn't quite caught up with this conversation. Should she be grateful that someone (an eighth-grader!) was talking to her? Or annoyed that the girl had been reading over her shoulder without permission?

"The *Telegraph*. The school newspaper," Elaine explained. "You haven't heard of it? Our first issue comes out next week, and we're always looking for good writers. From what I just saw, it looks like you can string a sentence together."

"Oh. Um, yeah," Gladys said.

Elaine raised a dark eyebrow. "Well, on paper at least. Might have to work on the conversationl skills if you want to be assigned interviews."

Something was pressing into Gladys's thigh—the buckle of the girl's messenger bag. A *green* messenger bag.

"Nice stuffed animal."

It all came flooding back. "I saw you at orientation!" Gladys blurted. "Except . . . isn't orientation for seventh-graders only?"

"Sharp observation skills!" Elaine nodded approvingly. "I was covering it for the paper. An interesting story could break at any time. You know—*Rising Seventh-Grader Wets His Pants, Has to Call Home for Mommy*." She let out a laugh that sounded more like a cackle.

Gladys sensed that Elaine expected her to laugh along, but she didn't. "You wouldn't actually publish an article like that, would you?" she asked. "The school wouldn't let you."

Elaine sighed and leaned in closer, lowering her voice conspiratorially. "Sadly, you're right. Freedom of the press has some real limits in an institution like this. But we have to keep pushing the boundaries." She sat up a little straighter. "You seem to have a critical eye about things here—I think you'd be a great addition to our staff."

Gladys wondered whether Elaine would have said the same thing if she had still been carrying her "stuffed animal" backpack. "Thanks for the offer," she said, trying to be diplomatic, "but my after-school schedule's already pretty full."

At this, Elaine's warm caramel demeanor seemed to harden into peanut brittle. "Seriously? The *Tele-*

graph is a prestigious publication; most student writers don't make the cut. You're turning down a rare opportunity here."

"Sorry," Gladys said, "but I just don't have time." She wished that she felt brave enough to say the real reason—"*I don't want to join because you don't seem like a very nice person*"—but given how touchy Elaine was already acting, Gladys preferred not to provoke her any further.

"Well, that's too bad," Elaine retorted. "But if you change your mind, we meet on Mondays in the Media Room after school." She pushed her chair back. "What's your name, by the way? Oh, never mind—there it is on your book."

Gladys felt her neck burn as Elaine read from the cover of her new notebook. "*This reviewing journal belongs to: Gladys Gatsby.* Well, hope to see you around, Gladys." She stood up and slung her messenger bag over her shoulder.

Hope to see you nowhere, Gladys thought as Elaine marched off.

The awkward conversation had made Gladys lose what little appetite she had, but she forced herself to finish her soup in the few remaining minutes of the lunch period anyway. She knew she wouldn't have another chance to eat until the end of the day. If there was one thing all her teachers had agreed on so far, it was that there were no snacks allowed in class.

★★★★

When the bell rang at the end of seventh period, everyone made their way through the halls to the auditorium for the special assembly. It was a mob scene, but Gladys managed to catch sight of Charissa and Parm exiting their English classroom together. Charissa was whispering something in Parm's ear, and Parm was actually laughing. Gladys was surprised, but pleased, to see the two of them getting along.

"Hey, guys," she said, walking up to them. "Wanna head down to the auditorium together?"

Parm immediately stopped laughing and glanced at her shoes. It was as if she was embarrassed to have been caught in the midst of such merriment, especially with a girl she allegedly did not like.

Charissa, though, was more chipper. "Gladys!" she cried. "Yes, absolutely! Marti and Ro are gonna meet me down there, too. We can all sit together!" She took a few steps ahead, leading the way to the stairs.

"Great," Parm grumbled, sidling up close to Gladys. "Eighth period is one of the only times of day I'm supposed to be able to escape from her."

In the auditorium, Charissa blocked off an entire row of seats, laying her backpack, cardigan, and even one of her shoes out to keep potential interlopers at bay. Since the row she had picked was the first row, though, there wasn't a lot of competition.

"Seriously, Charissa?" Parm asked. "Right down

front? I was planning to use this time to relax before soccer tryouts—maybe grab a nap."

"Come on," Charissa said. "Whoever's speaking might really have something important to teach us, and by sitting up front, we'll get to bask in all that knowledge! Here, sit by me—I'll make sure you stay awake."

Parm grumbled again, but took the seat next to Charissa anyway; Gladys knew well that sometimes it was easier to just give in to Charissa's demands than find the energy to debate her. Gladys slid in next to Parm, and Marti and Rolanda scooted in on Charissa's other side a few moments later, passing the lavender sweater and purple clog back to Charissa as they took their seats.

When everyone had settled down, Dr. Sloane took the stage. "Boys and girls," she announced, "it is my immense pleasure to welcome you to a special, inspirational presentation by one of the most exciting novelists of our time. Please put your hands together for thirteen-year-old literary phenom Mr. Hamilton Herbertson!"

At that moment, the boy Gladys hadn't seen or heard from since the end of summer camp strode across the DTMS stage, clad all in black and grinning from ear to ear.

Chapter 9

A SWIRL OF RAGE

GLADYS'S HEART THUDDED SO LOUDLY, she was sure her fellow seventh-graders could hear it all the way at the back of the auditorium—or would have been able to, if they hadn't been so noisy themselves. There were a lot of cheers from fans of Hamilton's best-selling novel, *Zombie-town, U.S.A.,* but also a few boos, probably from fellow Camp Bentley attendees. Hamilton's snooty opinions about the childishness of summer camp had not won him many fans there.

Gladys wasn't sure if she wanted to cheer or boo herself. She and Hamilton had exchanged phone numbers at the end of camp, but he had never called her. She'd told herself that he must be busy finishing up the sequel to his novel, and she knew how demanding deadlines could be. Several times, she had thought about calling, but in the end she'd always decided not to disturb him. Surely he would get in touch when he had time.

What if she had been wrong, though? If Hamilton had time to make a presentation at her school, he couldn't be *that* busy. Maybe he had decided that his friendship with Gladys wasn't worth continuing after all. In fact, he'd probably already forgotten about her.

Now Gladys felt an overwhelming urge to disappear. She slumped down in her seat and shook her hair forward into her face, though it would be hard to hide since she was sitting in the very first row.

Thanks a lot, Charissa.

Hamilton pulled a set of index cards from his black jeans pocket and cleared his throat in anticipation of his favorite activity: giving speeches.

"Thank you, Principal Sloane," his voice boomed into the microphone, "and thank you, students, for that enthusiastic welcome. I'm honored to be here in my adopted hometown of East Dumpsford, speaking to you all today."

He looked up from his cards, and Gladys cringed. Any moment now, he would spot her—and even though *he* had been the one to fall off the face of the earth, she still felt embarrassed. After all, she had thought their friendship meant more to him than it really did.

Hamilton glanced back at his notes before his eyes reached her side of the auditorium, and Gladys let out a small sigh of relief.

"I am here," he continued, "on this first day of school, to speak to you about the value of perseverance. Without it, I would not be one of the youngest number one *New York Standard* best-selling authors of all time. Now, in case you don't already know, *perseverance* is defined as . . ."

"Ugh!" Parm whispered as Hamilton pompously launched into a definition of the word. "He's so arrogant!"

"I know, right?" Charissa whispered back.

And there it was: mixed in with Gladys's annoyance and embarrassment, a pang of sympathy. Hamilton didn't *mean* to be so condescending; he had just never spent any time around other kids his age, so he had no idea how to act. She understood why Parm and Charissa would be offended by the way he talked down to them, since she'd felt that way once, too. But they just didn't know him the way she did—or the way she thought she had.

Opposing feelings were twisting together in Gladys's gut like a frozen-yogurt swirl. Relief to see Hamilton alive and well. Anger that he had not bothered to get in touch with her. Pity over his awful stage demeanor. Humiliation at thinking he'd forgotten her completely.

She had stopped listening to what he was actually saying, so she was surprised when the lights dimmed even further and the large screen behind him burst to life with the first slide of a multimedia presentation. Hamilton, a clicker in one hand and a microphone in the other, moved off to his right so as not to block the screen, bringing him to stand literally right in front of Gladys. Grateful now for the cover of darkness, she was able to observe her former friend as he clicked through pictures of himself signing books and droned on about following your dreams.

There was a picture of him at the Tipsy Typist restaurant, showing off the "Ham Herb" signature sandwich they had named after him. Gladys thought back to the ham-and-herbs sandwiches he had demanded from the Camp Bentley kitchen, and how she had gone out of her way to make some especially for him. Had he just used her to gain access to the camp's arugula supply?

Suddenly, her melty swirl of feelings crystallized into one single emotion: rage.

By the end of the summer, Gladys really had thought Hamilton had become a less selfish, more thoughtful person. But as she watched him now onstage, cocking his head to show off his stupid fedora and basking in the attention of his audience, she saw that she'd been wrong.

Hamilton Herbertson was still number one in his own book.

The lights came up after he clicked through his last slide—a shot of him alongside several foreign editions of his book—and the boy strode back to the center of the stage. "In conclusion," he said, returning his microphone to its stand, "you should strive hard toward achieving your goals and not let your young age stand in your way. After all, if I could do it . . . well, then at least one or two of you probably can, too."

Hamilton bowed, but before anyone could decide whether to applaud this final, backhanded nugget of wisdom, the bell rang out. Kids grabbed their bags, leapt to their feet, and turned away from their "inspirational speaker" to stream down the aisles.

Gladys followed, eager to be gone—but the exits were in the back of the room, and the aisles were jammed up in seconds. *Fudge.* She glanced back just in time to see Hamilton rise out of his bow, which reminded her of all the times he had swept off his fedora and bowed awkwardly to her at Camp Bentley. She let her gaze linger for a second too long, and Hamilton's eye caught hers.

"Gladys??"

At first, Gladys thought her name only sounded loud and echoey in her head, but then she realized Hamilton was still standing in front of the microphone. Her feet froze in place.

"Gladys!" he cried again. "It's really you!"

So he remembered her name, at least. And not only that, but it sounded like he was on the brink of sucking her in to his second-favorite activity: making an embarrassing scene. In fact, some of the kids who hadn't made it out of the auditorium yet were turning around now, and Parm—who had not attended Camp Bentley—stared at Gladys. "Wait a second," she hissed. "Do you *know* him?"

Charissa waggled her eyebrows at Gladys, then linked arms with Parm. "Come on," she told her. "I'll explain everything outside." Then, along with Marti and Rolanda, they slipped past Gladys and down the aisle.

At last, Gladys got her feet to wake up. *I've got to get out of here,* she thought. But the rear exit was still too far away. Making a split-second decision, she spun around and climbed the stairs that led to the stage instead.

The lights up there were surprisingly hot and bright; the faces of the students still in the auditorium all blurred together into one dark mass. She heard one titter rise from the audience, then another.

Fuuudge. Now she'd made it easier for everyone to stare at her. This had been a terrible decision.

"Gladys!" Hamilton said again, *still* talking into the microphone. "I've been dying to tell you—"

But she hadn't climbed up there to talk to him; he had already used, infuriated, and embarrassed her enough. She barreled past him into the wings, where she spotted an emergency exit. Without breaking her stride, she slammed through the heavy door.

Chapter 10

DON'T CHICKEN OUT

AS GLADYS STORMED DOWN THE SIDE
street that led away from school, she
considered the possibility of homeschooling more seriously than ever before. Her
parents both worked full-time, so there
was the small issue of who would teach
her . . . but Aunt Lydia could take care
of French lessons, and there were surely
online programs she could do for the rest
of it.

As long as she never had to show her
face at school again, she was game for
anything.

Well, except for the fact that *Hamilton*
was homeschooled, and Gladys really
didn't want to follow in that boy's foot-
steps. She could only imagine how pompously he would crow about being a leader
in educational trends if he found out.

Ugh. Why did every decision in her life have to be so complicated?

One choice was simple, at least: Gladys knew she wanted to get as far away from DTMS as possible. As she hoofed the long blocks to Mr. Eng's, she regretted not having ridden her bike that morning. She would have preferred to go straight home, but she'd promised her aunt she would stop in on her first day of work. And maybe, if things weren't too busy, they could start to plan for how to pull Gladys out of middle school for good.

The bell rang overhead as she pushed open the Gourmet Grocery's door. Gladys had expected things to be under better control now that Mr. Eng had help, but in fact, the shop looked worse than ever. The light was still out in the cheese fridge, two produce bins were empty, and the spice wall was partially dismantled. Standing in front of that wall having a discussion were Mr. Eng and Aunt Lydia—and Mr. Eng didn't sound happy.

"I simply asked you to restock the cinnamon," he said, "not to rearrange the entire wall!"

"I—I'm sorry," Aunt Lydia stammered. "I just had this vision of how nice the spices would look rearranged by color, and—"

"But that wasn't the task you were assigned!" Mr. Eng snapped. "The spices are arranged alphabetically so that customers can find them easily. Please put them back the way you found them, and then finish restocking."

Aunt Lydia stared at the tiles at her feet. "Of course."

Mr. Eng turned on his heel and stalked back into the storeroom; there were no other customers in the shop just then, and in the heat of the exchange, he hadn't even heard the bell over the door ring. Gladys was starting to wonder whether she could just back out of the store quietly when Aunt Lydia spotted her.

"My Gladiola!" She hastily wiped her eye, smudging eyeliner across her cheek in the process. Then, placing the bright yellow bottle of turmeric she was holding onto the nearest shelf—not the right one at all, Gladys noticed—she hurried over to hug her niece. "*Bonjour, bonjour!* How was your first day of school? My first day here has been *magnifique!*"

Clearly, Aunt Lydia was exaggerating; even if Gladys hadn't just overheard Mr. Eng scolding her, she looked exhausted and slightly disheveled. There was no way Gladys could now dump her own problems at her aunt's impractically sandaled, slightly swollen feet.

"Oh . . . my day was fine," Gladys lied. "I mean, a few bumps along the way, but nothing serious."

"That's my sweet star," Aunt Lydia said, giving her a squeeze. "Mature enough to handle anything life throws her way."

Gladys couldn't help but chafe at this undeserved praise. *Yeah, really mature,* she thought. *Ready to quit school just because someone embarrassed me!*

In any case, she was pretty sure that her aunt needed her help right now more than she needed her aunt's. "Hey, Aunt Lydia," Gladys said, "I don't really have any homework yet. How about I hang out here for a while and help you put this wall back together? Mr. Eng keeps the spices alphabetical, right? I can take *A* through *L*, and you take *M* through *Z*."

Aunt Lydia grunted something about alphabets being uncreative—but, to Gladys's relief, she agreed. "Thank you, my Gladragon. That would be a huge help."

Thirty minutes later, the spice wall was fixed, and Gladys had even coaxed her aunt into filling the empty bins by asking her what was supposed to be in them. When her aunt headed back to the storeroom for produce, Mr. Eng quickly emerged; it seemed he wasn't too keen on being in the same area as his new assistant.

When Gladys arrived home, Sandy was sitting on his front stoop, still in his school uniform. "Jeez, Gatsby, where've you been?" he cried. "I've been waiting out here for ages."

"Sorry," Gladys said, taking a seat beside him. "I

just . . . well . . . lots of first-day craziness. But how about you? Was the dragon fruit a hit?"

A crispy piece of Sandy's gelled hair came loose at his temple as he shook his head. "Turns out there's this new kid, Jonah; I guess he was basically the King of Gross at his old school. All through lunch, he kept telling stories about the disgusting stuff he ate last year. He actually laughed at my dragon fruit."

"Oh, no!" Gladys still felt kind of ambivalent about the whole idea of a grossness champion—but if there was going to be one, she wanted it to be Sandy.

"Yeah." He sighed. "And then, he pulled this . . . *thing* out of his lunch box. Have you ever heard of gefilte fish? It's basically a pale, slimy fish meatball. Jonah's family is half Jewish, and I guess they eat them during holidays. Anyway, he held it up for everyone to smell, and then, once all the other kids were completely grossed out by it, he ate it in one big bite."

"That doesn't seem fair," Gladys said. "He should have at least given you a chance to try some, too—you know, to prove he wasn't the only one brave enough to eat it."

"Yeah, well, that's what I said." Sandy pushed the rogue piece of hair back into place on his head. "I said he couldn't just waltz in and claim the title of Gross Foods King without giving other people a shot at a comeback. So then he said; 'Okay, let's have a rematch next week—whoever brings and eats the sickest thing on Monday wins for good.' He pretty much challenged me to a duel."

"So what did you say?" Gladys asked.

Sandy looked at her like she had just sprouted a second head. "I said yes, obviously! What, don't you think I can win?"

"Of course you can!" Gladys cried. "I didn't mean that. I just . . ." She thought about how she had run away from Hamilton earlier. "I guess head-on conflict isn't really my thing."

"Yeah, well, you can stay behind the scenes all you want on this," Sandy said, "but I'm definitely going to need your help. You know more about food than anyone, even my mom. What's the grossest thing you can think of?"

They spent the next few minutes brainstorming nasty-yet-edible school lunch ideas, and Gladys promised to save time that weekend to go on a yucky-food shopping spree together.

When she rose to return home, though, Gladys's brain circled back to what had happened at school. Sandy was bravely taking on his challenge, even though it might lead to some uncomfortable situations. Gladys, though, had chosen to turn her back on Hamilton rather than let him know why she was upset with him. She had chickened out. Was that really how she wanted to kick off her middle-school years—by running away from every complicated situation?

Gladys made her way up to her bedroom and scanned her bookshelf for her copy of *Zombietown, U.S.A.*, its black spine standing in a spot of honor between her other favorites: *Matilda* and the Harry Potter series.

She flipped it open to the inscription Hamilton had written on their last day of camp.

For Gladys,
   Chef, swimming coach, muse, and friend extraordinaire.
   Hamilton Herbertson

He had included his phone number under his name.

Gladys carried the book into the office, picked up the phone, and—before she could lose her nerve—dialed.

A voice-mail recording picked up on the first ring. "You've reached the Herbertsons. Please leave a message."

Gladys gulped. "Hey, Hamilton," she said after the beep. "Um, I'm sorry I ran off like that today. I'd like to talk to you, so . . . just give me a call when you have a chance. Bye."

She hung the receiver up gingerly; then, determined

not to waste the rest of her afternoon staring at it, headed to the kitchen and began pulling ingredients out for a baking project.

Since her aunt had arrived from Paris, Gladys had thought about attempting macarons, the notoriously delicate and tricky French sandwich cookies made with egg whites and almond flour. Aunt Lydia might still be missing her old life in Paris, but if Gladys did a good job, maybe the macarons would give her a taste of home.

She had just finished piping careful rounds of macaron batter onto a baking sheet when her parents arrived home from work.

"Well, well—what have we here?" Her dad placed his briefcase on the table and approached the baking sheet; Gladys had to shift her body to block him just as he was about to dunk an unwashed finger into one of her perfect circles.

"No way," she said. "You can try these when they're done, just like everyone else."

Her dad laughed, but when her mom spoke, her voice was noticeably cooler. "Cooking, Gladys? On the first night of school?"

"Well, I don't have any homework yet," Gladys said.

"Then I would think you might have time to hang out with some of your friends." Gladys's mom was always getting on her case about being more social;

sometimes she wondered if her mom was more paranoid about Gladys's friends dumping her than Gladys was.

"I saw Sandy earlier," Gladys told her, "and Parm and Charissa both had after-school activities." She left out the drama with Hamilton—her parents didn't need to know about that.

"After-school activities—now that sounds like fun," Gladys's dad said. "I still remember my first Debate Club meet in middle school . . . talk about adrenaline!"

Gladys nodded as politely as she could. Debate sounded almost as awful as Student Leadership Council, with the possible exception of a debate about the merits of superfine sugar versus confectioner's sugar. But somehow she doubted that was a topic on the debate team's agenda.

"Gladys," her mom said, "have a seat for a moment."

The macarons needed to rest before they went into the oven anyway, so Gladys followed her parents to the kitchen table.

"Honey," her mom started, "your dad and I have talked about this, and we think it would be best to impose some limits on your cooking during the school year. You know, to make sure you'll have plenty of time to meet new people, try new activities, and really get the most out of your middle-school experience."

"*What?*" Gladys couldn't believe her ears. The last

time her parents had restricted her cooking privileges, it was because she had started a fire in the kitchen. "But I didn't do anything wrong!"

"This isn't a punishment, Gladdy," her dad said. "It's just an effort to make sure you have a healthy balance in your schedule. Now, there must be some after-school activities you'll want to try in your spare time."

"There's just one," she said. "French Club. And that doesn't even start up until next week!"

"Then maybe you should find a few more," Gladys's mom suggested. "Or maybe a sports team you'd like to try out for?"

Gladys stared down at the fake-wood pattern of the kitchen table. She'd thought that her parents had made a lot of progress over the summer—that they'd really started to understand her passion for food and cooking. But this just proved that they didn't understand her at all.

"You can still finish your cookies tonight," her dad said, "but starting tomorrow, your kitchen access will be restricted to once a week."

"*Once* a week?" Gladys had a list of recipes to try that was almost three pages long. If she was only allowed to cook one time a week, it would take her years to perfect them all. "This is so unfair!"

"We thought you might feel that way," her mom said, "but we've discussed this, and we think it's for your own good. I bet you'll even thank us once you get more involved in other activities. You might find something else you love to do just as much as cooking!"

"But I already know what I love to do." Gladys could tell she was not going to win this battle, but she couldn't help trying anyway.

Her dad reached over and ruffled her hair. "Just give this a shot, kiddo. Don't be afraid of having new experiences."

Gladys found this statement particularly ironic coming from the man who'd been ordering the same exact chicken lo mein from Palace of Wong every week for the last nine years.

When her parents left the table, Gladys slumped back in her chair. Baking always helped her let off steam, and cooking new international dishes helped her prepare for her restaurant-reviewing trips. Now, in one fell swoop, her parents had taken away her ability to do both.

How on earth had she ever thought they were ready to hear about her secret job?

Relieved that she hadn't gone through with telling them weeks ago, Gladys got up to preheat the oven. In her unfocused state, though, she turned the temperature a bit too high, and when her macarons came out half an hour later, they had lost their shape and spread out on the pan, turning into what looked like slightly burnt, sticky fried eggs.

Gladys banged the pan onto the range top in frustration. Her cookies were ruined, and who knew when she would have a chance to try the recipe again?

She barely touched the quiche that an exhausted Aunt Lydia brought home from Mr. Eng's for dinner that night, and made a mental note to tell her aunt that she finally understood what it felt like to be too depressed to enjoy good food. But tonight wasn't the night for that; Aunt Lydia had had a trying day of her own.

"Lydia's first day of work and Gladys's first day of middle school," Gladys's mom crowed as she cleared the table. "It's new beginnings for everyone!"

Gladys heaved herself up from her chair and headed for the stairs. She made one last pit stop on the way to bed, to stare again hopefully at the phone in the office. If anyone she knew could commiserate about having parents who didn't get them, it was Hamilton. But as strongly as she willed him to return her call, the phone stayed silent.

Chapter 11

SNACKS FOR ZOMBIES

GLADYS HAD ALWAYS HEARD THAT THE first day at a new school was the hardest. But by the time she stumbled into French class the next afternoon with a backpack full of homework assignments, she thoroughly disagreed. Really, the first day was pretty easy, with all that seat shuffling and introducing; it was the second day when you started to do actual work.

At least her scene onstage the day before didn't seem to have made a big impression on her fellow students. In social studies, Charissa had reassured her that many of her classmates had already left the auditorium by the time she'd climbed up there, plus most people probably wouldn't recognize her even if they had seen her. Thankfully, it seemed that she was right. Gladys's status as a nobody at DTMS was still intact.

"*Bonjour,* class!" the teacher cried once the bell had rung. "My name is Madame Goldstein, and this is Introduction to French. Now, the first thing we must do is give you all new names."

"New names?" an unfamiliar boy called out. "What's wrong with our old ones?"

The class tittered, and Madame Goldstein smiled. "This is a French class, so we must all have French names! I will take attendance, and after I call out each of your names, I will suggest a French name for you. If you like it, then that will become your name in this class. *D'accord?*"

Gladys and her classmates nodded.

"*Bon.* Now, first we have Amanda Abbey? There you are. How about Amandine?" Madame Goldstein said the new name with a beautiful accent, and Amanda nodded eagerly. "*Très bien,*" Madame Goldstein said. "Very good." And she spelled Amanda's new name out on the chalkboard.

She continued to call attendance—a boy named Ryan became Rolande, Charissa became Charisse.

"Gladys Gatsby?" Madame Goldstein called. Gladys felt her breath catch and slowly raised her hand. "Ah, *bon.* How about . . . Giselle?"

Giselle—that sounded lovely. "*Merci beaucoup,*" Gladys said, using the phrase for "thank you very much" that she had learned from her aunt.

Madame's thin eyebrows shot up. "Does our Giselle already know some *français*?"

"Oh, just a few words," Gladys said, embarrassed that she'd said anything. "My aunt lived in Paris for a long time."

"Well, I hope you'll be joining our French Club, then!" Madame Goldstein said. "In fact, I hope you all will. It's a wonderful chance to learn more about French culture and get in a little extra language practice. And every year, we take a field trip to a French restaurant in New York City . . ." Madame sighed. "Well, this year, our club will have to brainstorm some new ideas for funding such a trip. Our first meeting will be next week."

An outing to a French restaurant in the city sounded wonderful; Gladys was determined to help the club make sure the outing could still happen.

Once everyone in the class had been rechristened, Madame Goldstein asked them to rearrange their seats in alphabetical order by their new French names. But first, she taught everyone how to ask what someone else's name was in French, and how to answer. Then they were turned loose to figure out what order they belonged in.

It was a lot of fun, and by the end of the lesson, Gladys was pretty sure she had a new favorite teacher.

After class, Gladys headed to her locker to pack

up. Between all the heavy books now weighing down her blue backpack and the fact that she hadn't eaten since brunch time, she felt slightly dizzy. She wasn't the only one, either—a lot of the other kids around her looked like exhausted zombies as they tottered toward the school exit, and she overheard more than one complain about being hungry. "I'd gnaw someone's face off for a brownie right now," one boy muttered to his friend.

Gladys wasn't sure about the face-gnawing, but something sweet *did* sound pretty appealing right now. She was debating whether to stop at Mr. Eng's for a fresh-baked cookie or head straight home to see if Hamilton had called when Parm came flying up to her.

"I made it!" she cried. "I'm a starter on the soccer team!"

Gladys's backpack fell to the ground with a thud. "That's terrific!" she cried. "Congrats!" She threw her arms around her friend, who could barely stay still long enough to be hugged.

"I really didn't know how I did at tryouts," Parm said breathlessly, "but the list just got posted. Almost all the other starters are eighth-graders. I can't believe it! Okay, I'd better run or I'll be late for drills, plus Coach said she had to talk to us about fund-raising today. I hope she has a good idea for how to get us to the tournament—I *really* want to go!"

Gladys grinned at Parm; it was nice to see her so excited.

"Call me later and let me know how your first practice went," Gladys said.

As Parm turned to leave, Gladys's empty stomach gave a particularly ferocious growl—which gave her an idea.

"Parm!" she cried, and her friend whirled around—as did several other kids at their lockers. Gladys shrank from their stares, but took a step closer to her friend. "Bake sale," she whispered.

"Huh?"

"If you need a fund-raising idea," Gladys elaborated, "I think an after-school bake sale could make a lot of money. Especially for the kids who have fourth-period lunch—we're starving!"

Comprehension dawned in Parm's brown eyes. "Great idea! You know that *I* still think most desserts are gross, but I can see how other people might want to buy them. Thanks, Gladys!" She took off then, expertly dodging the kids in her way as her feet dribbled a ghost soccer ball down the hall.

Gladys shook her head. In elementary school, Parm had only ever eaten two things—plain spaghetti and cold cereal with milk—and it sounded like she was still as picky as ever. But Gladys was glad she had liked her idea. An after-school bake sale couldn't come soon enough.

The phone rang that night just as Gladys was getting into her pajamas, and her heart leapt—maybe Hamilton was getting back to her at last! Her father called her to the phone a moment later, but when she picked up, the voice on the other end belonged not to Hamilton but to Parm.

"Hey," Parm said. "Sorry I didn't call sooner—my parents made me sit with them through their entire dinner, even though all I ate was one bowl of noodles." Parm sounded annoyed—more than her family dinner situation warranted.

"Is something wrong?" Gladys asked.

Parm sighed. "Well, yeah. At practice, Coach asked for fund-raising plans, and I mentioned your bake sale idea—"

"Oh, no—she didn't like it?" Gladys asked. "I'm sorry."

"No, no, Coach loved it, and so did everyone else." Parm sounded glummer than ever.

"Oh," Gladys replied. "So what's the problem?"

"They want *me* to be in charge of it!" Parm burst out. "I'm supposed to come up with the recipes and organize the team to get the baking done. I think Coach assumed that since I brought the idea up, I must . . . you know . . . *like* to bake. She said she was gonna try to set up a series of sales, with the first one scheduled for next Monday. But to get ready for the first game of the season, we've got practice every day after school *plus* Saturday and Sunday! So I don't know when I'd even have time, but it doesn't matter. You know I can't cook." She groaned. "I'll just have to tell her tomorrow that I can't do it."

A grin was starting to spread across Gladys's face. "No way," she said. "You may not be the world's best baker—yet—but you've got a friend who can help you."

"I couldn't ask you to do that," Parm said. "You suggested this to help me out, not to get pulled into a ring of soccer-baking madness."

Gladys laughed. "You forget that I actually *like* to cook. And anyway," she said, lowering her voice, "right now my parents are only letting me use the kitchen once a week. So if you let me come over to *your* house for a baking project, you'd actually be doing me a favor."

"I'd be doing *you* a favor?" Parm sounded skeptical. "Okay, I mean this in the most loving way possible, Gladys, but . . . you're a weirdo."

Gladys grinned. "A weirdo with all the skills you need. What time does your practice end on Sunday?"

"One o'clock," Parm said.

"Then have the team meet me at Mr. Eng's at one fifteen," she said. "We'll buy the ingredients, then bake at your house. Who knows—maybe you'll even enjoy it!"

Gladys could practically hear Parm wince at the

other end of the line, but she agreed to the plan. "Okay—thanks a jillion. Maybe this won't be a complete disaster after all."

Gladys sauntered off to bed after hanging up, visions of soccer-ball-iced cookies dancing in her head. She couldn't wait for the weekend.

Chapter 12

BODACIOUSLY FUNKY

THAT THURSDAY NIGHT, SITTING OUT ON the porch, Aunt Lydia told Gladys that she'd had a phone call while Gladys was at school.

"A call for me?" Gladys interrupted before her aunt could say more. "What did he—I mean, who was it?"

Aunt Lydia gave her a funny look. "No, it wasn't for you, my Gladiola. It was for me, from Mr. Eng. He wants me to come in on Saturday and work all day to help with the weekend crowds. See, I told you I did a good job on my first day there!"

"Oh." Gladys tried not to let her disappointment show. It had been three days now since she'd left Hamilton that message—why hadn't he called her back? "That's great," she told her aunt. "More work means more savings, right?"

"Right," Lydia said. She lowered her voice. "But that means we won't be able to go eat in Queens that day. I'm sorry."

"Oh—that's okay." Gladys still wanted to try her hand at some Salvadoran cooking before heading to that restaurant, so unless Parm wanted to sell pupusas (traditional stuffed cornmeal pancakes) at her team's bake sale, she was pretty sure she'd have to wait for her cooking day at home next week to make some. Putting off their reviewing trip until the next weekend meant that Gladys would be cutting it close to get her review in on time, but she'd worked on tight deadlines before.

"You just focus on doing a good job at Mr. Eng's," she told her aunt. "You know, do what he asks and try not to cause trouble."

"Trouble? *Moi?*" Aunt Lydia harrumphed. "I would never!"

The school week finished off with an announcement from Madame Goldstein that the French Club would hold its inaugural meeting the following *mardi* (Tuesday). Several of Gladys's classmates seemed happy to hear this news, but Charissa waved a distressed hand in the air.

"Madame!" she cried. "Student Leadership Council already meets on Tuesdays. Next week we're having our officer election!"

Madame frowned. "I am sorry to hear that, Charisse. But this is the only time that works for us. Perhaps you can switch off between the two, every other week?"

As the bell rang, Charissa sank back into her seat, pouting. "I already have to switch off between Mathletes and debate on Wednesdays," she told Gladys. "Plus I've still got dance class, gymnastics, tennis, and horseback! And, you know, homework."

"Sounds like you might be overcommitted," Gladys said.

"You say that like it's a bad thing."

Charissa made Gladys agree to call her the next Tuesday night and tell her about everything she'd missed from the first French Club meeting. "And could you get me any handouts, too?" she said, glancing up at the wall clock. "Shoot, I'm gonna be late for tennis. Have a good weekend, Giselle!"

Gladys spent Saturday morning searching online for recipes for the soccer bake sale and planning out a list of ingredients. She also raided the kitchen for the right kinds of baking utensils and pans. She was happy to have access to Aunt Lydia's things, since her own collection was not complete.

Then, that afternoon, she and Sandy headed to Mr. Eng's to shop for ingredients for the next battle in the War of Gross Foods.

"You don't think he sells fried crickets, do you?"

Sandy asked. "I was doing some research online, and people eat them for snacks in Cambodia. One blogger said they tasted just like popcorn . . . only with legs that sometimes get stuck in your teeth."

"I don't know," Gladys told him. "I mean, Mr. Eng imports a lot of interesting stuff, but I don't think I've ever seen any bugs there."

When they reached the shop, things seemed even more chaotic than they had been on Gladys's last few visits. The aisles were crowded, shelves were half bare, and Mr. Eng was fielding a line ten customers deep at the cash register. But instead of hurrying around to help customers or restock, Aunt Lydia was standing near the door, a large plate of cheese in her hand.

"Free sample?" she asked customers as they entered the store. "Would you like to try our new Danish blue? It's very robust."

Customers, of course, stopped to try the cheese, which was creating a bottleneck at the store's narrow entrance. Gladys noticed that the light in the cheese refrigerator was *still* out, though it seemed that half of that fridge's contents were now cubed or sliced up on Aunt Lydia's sample platter.

"Gladys! Sandy!" Aunt Lydia cried. "*Bienvenue!* Would you like to try some cheese?"

"Yeah!" Sandy cried, barreling straight over. "Which one's the grossest?"

Aunt Lydia looked slightly taken aback by this

question, but recovered quickly. "Well, this aged Limburger is rather bodaciously funky, if that's what you're looking for . . ."

She grabbed a toothpick from the tray and speared Sandy a generous chunk. He sniffed at it and almost gagged. "Oh, yeahhhh," he said. "That's the stuff!"

Though she was happy to see Aunt Lydia help Sandy find a food for his battle, Gladys was also concerned at the amount of food her aunt was giving away for free. "Um, Aunt Lydia," she said quietly. "Did Mr. Eng ask you to hand out samples?"

"Technically, no," her aunt responded, passing a toothpick of sharp cheddar to another customer, "but I'm sure he'll appreciate my taking the initiative. Well, if he ever makes it out from behind that register, that is. I'm afraid I might run out of samples and have to cut some more up before he even notices!"

Gladys highly doubted Mr. Eng would be pleased if he did find a moment to spot what was going on. "You know what?" she said, trying to keep her voice light. "I think you've been generous enough. I mean, you'll want to leave some cheese for the customers to *buy,* right? Speaking of which, it'd be great if they could see well enough to read the labels. Did you notice that the light in the cheese fridge is out?"

Aunt Lydia glanced over in the fridge's direction and frowned. "Hmm. Someone really ought to change that bulb."

Yes, someone should, Gladys thought exasperatedly. *You!*

Gladys loved her aunt, but she couldn't ignore the fact that she did not seem to be doing anything Mr. Eng asked of her. Had she been this bad at listening to her new boss's orders at the café in Paris? Gladys had been sure that the new owners were horrible people and that her aunt was in the right to quit in a huff. But now, after witnessing Aunt Lydia's behavior at work multiple times, she wasn't so sure.

"Here—why don't you let me and Sandy handle the sample tray for a few minutes while you go change that light?" she suggested. "I think Mr. Eng keeps spare bulbs back in the storeroom."

"Okay, okay," Aunt Lydia said, "but make sure you push the Limburger."

"'Bodaciously funky'—yeah, right," Sandy muttered as Aunt Lydia moved away. "It's unpopular because it tastes like a foot!" He grabbed another sample and held it out to a man entering the store. "Excuse me, sir, but would you like to try some Limburger? It's vomitously delicious!" The man gave Sandy a strange look, and Gladys couldn't help but laugh as he hurried away.

"You're terrible," she said.

"No, *this* is terrible." He waved the sample under Gladys's nose, and her eyes watered. "I'm gonna win on Monday for *sure.*"

A few minutes later, the cheese fridge was bathed in glorious light, the sample platter was bare (thanks, in most part, to Sandy, who forced down several more bites of Limburger "to build up tolerance"), and Mr. Eng was none the wiser. Still, as Sandy lined up to buy his package of putrescent cheese, Gladys couldn't help wondering how many times she was going to have to swoop in and save her aunt from her self-destructive instincts at work.

Luckily, Aunt Lydia wasn't on duty the next day when Gladys returned to the Gourmet Grocery to meet Parm and her teammates. Still in their practice clothes, the girls peeled off in groups of two or three to troll the aisles for the ingredients Gladys assigned them. Somehow, talking to kids she didn't know was less scary when the subject was food.

Parm, however, did seem a little scared. "How many different things are we making??" she asked, her voice panicky as she looked over Gladys's list.

"I thought we'd do three recipes." Gladys showed Parm the first recipe she had printed. "The frosting pattern on these cookies makes them look like soccer balls, see? Then there's this brownie recipe I got from Sandy's mom, because kids love chocolate and her brownies are the best. And then, finally, I wanted to make something gluten-free, for the kids who can't eat wheat." Gladys shuffled to a new page. "I did a bunch of searching and finally came up with these Indian confections made with chickpea flour."

Parm looked at the picture on Gladys's printout. "I know those. There's a sweets shop in Jackson Heights where my family likes to go sometimes, and they sell them. But wait! Don't they have some kind of nasty name?" Parm looked at the paper again, then pointed to the subtitle. "Yeah, that's it: barfi."

Gladys nodded. "I thought maybe we'd just keep the name to ourselves until *after* the kids had tried them."

"Good plan," Parm said. "I'm sure it actually means something else anyway, right?"

"I looked it up, and it comes from the Hindi word for 'snow,'" Gladys told her. "Now come on, let's get these last few ingredients."

Their bill at Mr. Eng's was not cheap, but Gladys promised the team they would make plenty more in profits the next day. "The good thing about selling three different items is that kids will want to try them all, so hopefully you'll get more than one sale per kid," Gladys said. Parm agreed that that made sense.

At Parm's, under Gladys's watchful eye, everyone rolled up their sleeves and busted out the mixing bowls. Pretty soon, Gladys could tell who was better at making precise measurements and who was better suited to more physical work, like cracking eggs and mixing dough. With eighteen girls working hard on their different tasks, it didn't take long before there were several trays of cookies baking in the oven, multiple pans of brownie batter on deck, and another large tray of barfi batter firming up in the refrigerator.

The trickiest part of the entire dessert-making adventure would be icing the cookies so they would look like soccer balls. Gladys had found a video online for how to stretch dots of black icing into pentagon shapes using toothpicks, and she demonstrated for Parm and her teammates on a cooled cookie. It was painstaking work, but the results looked pretty good. Soon, five of the most artistic girls on the team were hard at work on the designs.

At one point, Parm's older brother Jagmeet wandered into the kitchen. A few self-conscious giggles arose from the bakers, but Jagmeet definitely seemed more interested in the food than in the girls. "Cookies! Nice," he said, and reached for the one Parm had just finished decorating. Gladys had never heard her friend scream so loud—or seen Jagmeet, who was a star basketball player at Dumpsford Township High, run so fast.

Parm had taken a few deep breaths to calm herself down before she realized that Gladys, her teammates, and her mother, who had recently joined them in the kitchen, were all staring at her. "What?" she snapped. "Each of these takes five minutes to decorate! No way was I gonna let him steal one."

Her mother smiled. "It's nice to see you taking pride in your work, Parminder."

When her mom stepped away from them, Parm shook her head. "Don't be fooled," she said quietly to Gladys. "She's just hoping that *I'll* steal one of these cookies. Which I will *not*. Mom still thinks that one of these days I'm gonna wake up and like eating all sorts of things I didn't like the day before. She's living in a fantasy world."

At that, Gladys couldn't help but think of her own parents. "Hey, you don't think your mom will tell whoever picks me up that we were cooking here, do you?" she asked. "Because my parents are *also* living in a fantasy world—one where they think access to the kitchen once a week is enough for me."

"I'll make sure she's busy when your ride comes," Parm promised, and Gladys would have hugged her if Parm hadn't been in the middle of decorating another soccer-ball cookie.

Eventually, the icing on the cookies was set, the brownies were cooled, and the barfi was solidified and cut into tasty-looking cubes. The team agreed to set prices for the items according both to size and the effort it had taken to prepare them: the barfi cubes would sell for a dollar apiece, the brownies for two dollars, and the soccer-ball cookies for three dollars.

"That way, there are also different price points for students who have different amounts of money with them," Parm pointed out. Gladys was impressed—her friend really was getting into the spirit of the bake sale now.

They had just finished wrapping all the goods in plastic when Gladys's dad honked his horn outside. Parm immediately moved off into the living room to distract her mother so she wouldn't head outside to talk to Mr. Gatsby, and Gladys quickly reloaded her blue backpack with the cooking tools she'd brought over. She still missed her lobster, but she had to admit that the new bag had a lot more capacity.

Gladys collapsed into the station wagon's backseat a few minutes later. It had felt like fun in the moment, but now the exhaustion of directing three separate baking projects for several hours seemed to hit her all at once. How did professional pastry chefs do it, day after day? Gladys thought of Classy Cakes, the "dessert bistro" in Manhattan that had been the subject of her very first review for the *Standard*. Her review had been positive, but even so, she wondered if she'd given the bakers enough credit.

Gladys's eyelids had just started drooping when her father slammed on the car brakes. "What the . . . ?"

They were in the parking lot of Pathetti's Pies—or, what had been Pathetti's Pies. Gladys shook the sleep from her eyes as her dad jumped out of the car. The sign overhead, with pizza pies inside each giant *P*, had been taken down, and the building looked abandoned.

Gladys followed her dad to the building's front door. Where the restaurant's hours had been posted, now there was only a sign that said PROPERTY FOR LEASE BY OWNER, CALL BOB. A phone number was listed underneath.

"I can't believe this," Gladys's dad said, shaking his head. "I mean, I knew that business was getting slower for them, but now they're just . . . gone? Our favorite pizza place!"

"Sorry, Dad." Pathetti's certainly wasn't *Gladys's* favorite pizza place—she could do a much better job with her own homemade dough and fresh toppings. But she knew that her parents loved it, so she felt at least a little bad for their loss. "But hey, maybe something better will come in!"

"Better than Pathetti's??" Her dad's head shook as he spoke. "Impossible."

He was still muttering about it fifteen minutes later when they arrived home with sacks from Sticky Burger. "I thought we were having pizza," Gladys's mom said, and her dad filled her in on the bad news.

"For lease by owner? That means he doesn't have a real estate agent," Gladys's mom murmured. "*I* could be his real estate agent and handle the leasing process for him! Did you write the number down, George?"

"Write it down? Of course not," Gladys's dad said. "I was too busy thinking about how I'd never have another triple-cheese-and-bacon pizza again!"

Gladys's mom made an exasperated noise, and a few moments later she was heading out to the car. "I'll be back!" she called, and drove off in the direction of the former Pathetti's Pies.

It was at that moment that Gladys realized she hadn't seen her aunt since they'd come into the house—but she heard the TV playing in the den. She made her way back to that room, where she found Aunt Lydia in her old position on the couch in her sweats and stained T-shirt, staring listlessly at the screen.

"Aunt Lydia!" Gladys cried. "What's wrong?"

Her aunt turned to her with tears in her eyes. "Oh, my Gladiola," she said. "Your auntie has lost her job again."

Chapter 13

TASTE TEST

"LOST YOUR JOB?" GLADYS CRIED. "But . . . how? When? You didn't even work today!"

"Mr. Eng called," Aunt Lydia said glumly. "He didn't fire me outright, but he said that when I come in tomorrow, we need to have a 'serious discussion about my future at the store.' That's almost exactly what the new owners of the café in Paris said before . . ." Her voice trailed off.

Gladys had to agree that this didn't sound too good. Maybe Mr. Eng had noticed how much expensive cheese was missing from his display case . . . but even if he hadn't, he knew by now that her aunt wasn't the most focused worker.

Then again, Mr. Eng was a reasonable man. Maybe, if Aunt Lydia really made a commitment to doing better, he would give her another chance.

Aunt Lydia sighed. "It's probably for the best," she said. "Now we can just call Fiona and tell her that we'll—I mean, *Gladys* will—take that full-time restaurant-reviewing job."

"But . . ." Gladys's voice cracked. With so much else going on this week, she had pushed the job situation to the back of her mind. She certainly didn't feel ready to make any permanent decisions about it. There had to be another solution to this situation—at least a temporary one.

"But the *Standard* job wouldn't start until January," she said, "and it's only September! I thought you wanted to save up some money. And won't you get bored if you're stuck in this house until then with nothing to do?"

Aunt Lydia glanced over at the TV, then down at the open bag of chips on the table. "I suppose so."

"Come on, then," Gladys said in her most rousing voice. "You have to fight for your job! Just try a little harder to follow Mr. Eng's directions at work, and everything will be fine."

A small smile crossed her aunt's face. "All right," she said. "I can try."

Gladys forced herself to smile back. "Great. So, uh, what time does Mr. Eng want you to come in tomorrow?"

"Eight o'clock," Aunt Lydia said.

Then I'll be there at seven twenty, Gladys thought. It wasn't that she didn't trust her aunt to save her own job—but she figured a little extra help couldn't hurt.

The next morning, Gladys rode her bike so that she would have time to make a detour to the Gourmet Grocery before school. She caught Mr. Eng just as he was unlocking the security gate.

"Good morning, Gladys!" he said. The gate made a *rap-bap-bap-bap* noise as it rose to reveal the glass door behind it. "You're here very early."

"Middle school starts earlier than elementary," Gladys told him, parking her bike.

"And it's in the opposite direction," Mr. Eng said with a wink. "So this must be a special trip for you. Come on in."

Inside, the store was dark and silent, and Gladys imagined the groceries sleeping quietly in their bins and on their shelves. Then Mr. Eng flipped a switch; the fluorescent lights overhead came on with a buzz, and all around her the muted tones of fruits and vegetables and spices burst into vibrant life.

"Mr. Eng," Gladys said, suddenly energized. "You can't fire my aunt today."

"Ah, I thought that's what this might be about." Mr. Eng dropped his keys on the counter and leaned forward on it. "I'm sorry, Gladys, but she's just not a good worker. I've given her two full trial days, which I really think is more than fair."

Gladys's stomach bottomed out. She had half hoped that Mr. Eng would tell her she was crazy and that he had no intention of firing Aunt Lydia. But for once, the awful thing that Gladys had suspected was exactly the thing that was in danger of happening.

"I don't mean to hurt you or your family," Mr. Eng continued, and indeed, his voice sounded the opposite of callous. "This is a business decision, not a personal one. Having your aunt here has made me realize that I really do need an assistant at the shop; it just needs to be someone who can follow orders."

"I know that she's made some mistakes," Gladys said hurriedly, "but she's still adjusting to life in America. If you could just give her a little more time—"

But Mr. Eng was shaking his head. "I need someone here whom I can trust to run the store entirely in my absence," he said. "I've registered for several trade shows over the next couple of months. They're like big conventions with lots of different types of food products on display and available for sampling so attendees can find new products to sell in their stores," he explained. "But they're all on Saturdays, and weekends are now the busiest time here. I just don't feel I can trust your aunt to hold down the fort on a Saturday."

Gladys sighed. If she was honest with herself, she couldn't really picture her aunt managing the shop alone, either. But what she could easily picture was her aunt hurrying around from one booth to another at a convention, snatching up samples and making decisions about which variety of artisan cracker or balsamic vinegar tasted the best.

"What if you sent Aunt Lydia to the trade shows?" Gladys said.

Mr. Eng, who was now breaking a fresh roll of quarters into the cash register drawer, looked up. "What?"

"She loves samples," Gladys said. Mr. Eng grimaced, and Gladys realized that maybe that hadn't been the best example to bring up. "I mean, she has a great palate. And like you just said, she's always flitting from one thing to the next. Who better to send off to taste-test food at a big convention on your behalf?"

"She did impress me with her knowledge of cheeses and spices when I first met her . . ." Mr. Eng said slowly. "Plus, those conventions *do* require a lot of walking. And on these old knees . . ."

Gladys could tell that she was making progress. It was time to drive her point home. "And you know that I'm good at doing research and taking notes," she added, "so I could work with her at home and make sure she has a good system for keeping track of the stuff she tries! Maybe I could even go with her to the first one to help out."

Now a hint of a smile played across Mr. Eng's face. "This is not a terrible idea, Gladys," he said. "All right—I'm willing to send her to the first convention and see how she does. If I'm happy with her work, she can represent the store at the others. But once they wrap up in October, that will be the end of your aunt's employment here. Business is doing better now, for sure, but I still can't afford to throw money away."

"I understand," Gladys said quietly. She hadn't fixed things forever, but at least she had saved her aunt's job for a little while longer. *And maybe,* she thought, *if Aunt Lydia does really well, she'll persuade Mr. Eng to reconsider.*

Gladys's classes seemed to drag by that day as she waited for the final bell and Parm's bake sale.

She ran into Parm in the hallway after third period, and her friend assured her that the baked goods were safe in the teachers' break room, where she had gotten special permission to store them. "And me and three of the other girls have a pass to get out of class fifteen minutes early to set up," Parm told her, "so things should be all ready by the time the last bell rings."

"Super," Gladys said. "I'll come down as soon as French lets out."

But at the end of French class, Madame Goldstein called Gladys up to her desk.

"Giselle, a word, *s'il vous plaît,*" she said.

Gladys and Charissa exchanged a glance; what could this be about? "I'd wait for you outside, but I've gotta get to gymnastics," Charissa whispered as Gladys stood up.

"No worries," Gladys replied. "But hey, make sure you stop in the lobby on your way—there are gonna be some awesome desserts for sale today."

"Ooh, thanks!" Charissa slung her purple backpack over one shoulder and sauntered out of the classroom after the other kids.

Gladys approached her teacher's desk. "Yes, Madame?" she said.

Madame smiled. "Giselle, I believe that we have a good friend in common."

"We—we do?" Gladys was completely baffled now. What was her teacher talking about?

"Oui," Madame replied. "This person is actually my neighbor. It is someone who is extremely fond of you."

Gladys's own heart took a tiny leap. Could it be Hamilton? His family had only moved to the area at the beginning of the summer; she didn't know which part of town they lived in, but they must be neighbors with her French teacher. She almost let out a giddy laugh. What were the odds?

"This person," Madame continued, "just learned that you are in my class, and asked if I would pass a letter along to you." She held out a sealed white envelope; her thumb was covering up part of the writing, but Gladys spotted her own last name on it in neat block letters. "*Excusez-moi* for being so mysterious, but the writer asked that I not reveal any more—and also told me to make it clear that I was ignorant of the letter's contents, as they might be considered somewhat personal."

Considered somewhat personal—that sounded like Hamilton, all right.

Gladys accepted the letter with a trembling hand. So *that* was why he hadn't called her back; he'd wanted to write to her instead. It was such a grand, old-fashioned gesture that she was almost willing to forgive all of his past transgressions right then and there.

Almost.

Gladys was dying to rip right into the envelope, but if there was "personal" content . . . well, it would be better if she could take it somewhere private. She had been looking forward to the bake sale all day, but now she couldn't wait to get home.

"*Merci*, Madame," Gladys said.

"*De rien*," Madame replied.

And with that, Gladys burst out of the classroom with more energy than she had ever been able to summon at the end of a day of middle school.

Chapter 14

A FULL PLATE

OKAY, GLADYS TOLD HERSELF AS SHE barreled down the hallway. *I'll stop REALLY fast to see Parm, then go straight home to look at the letter.* She rounded a corner and picked up speed.

The halls were weirdly empty, but Gladys soon found out where all the kids were: the bake sale. The table of treats was absolutely mobbed, and even with three other team members on hand to help, it looked like Parm was barely keeping up with demand. Gladys recognized several kids from her lunch period pushing toward the front of the line, including Elaine de la Vega, who Gladys knew was supposed to be at the *Telegraph* meeting. She had to smile; she'd been right to predict that a bake sale would be a big hit with the early lunchers.

The soccer-ball-shaped cookies were by far the most popular item; in fact, by the time Gladys squeezed her way up to the table, there was only one left.

"Hey, Parm, how much for that cookie?" the boy next to Gladys asked. She recognized his voice—it was Owen Green, who had gotten Parm embroiled in a food fight in the East Dumpsford Elementary cafeteria the year before.

"Three dollars," Parm said automatically, but when she looked up and saw who had asked, her eyes narrowed. "Oh—for you? *Four* dollars."

Owen grunted, but dug into his pocket anyway. "Okay."

"Wait!" cried a voice, and a round-cheeked girl pushed her way forward. "Don't sell it to him. I'll give you five dollars for it."

"What?" Owen spluttered. "No fair!"

"I'll give you six bucks!" another voice shouted from the crowd.

"Seven!"

"Forty-two!"

The crowd hushed at that offer, then split as Charissa Bentley glided forward, bills fanned out in her hand like a peacock's display.

"Aaaand, sold!" Parm cried. She accepted Charissa's money to a chorus of groans. "Sorry, guys, but this *is* a fund-raiser. And hey, there are still plenty of brownies and barf—I mean, *gluten-free sweet squares*—left."

She passed Charissa her soccer-ball cookie with a smile. Maybe, Gladys thought, her two best school friends really might be starting to like each other.

At Gladys's left, Elaine de la Vega was snapping pictures of the bake sale goodies with a small camera. "Excuse me," she said to Parm, "but I don't think DTMS has ever seen such a successful fund-raiser before. This is a newsworthy event! Do you have a few minutes for an interview with the *Telegraph*?"

Parm passed a "sweet square" over to another paying customer. "Um, we're a little busy right now," she replied. "But the person you really should talk to is Gladys Gatsby. She picked out the recipes and oversaw all the baking. And actually, the whole sale was her idea in the first place! There she is." Gladys didn't even have time to think about ducking away before Parm pointed her out.

Elaine's camera flashed as she whirled around; her finger must have accidentally depressed the button in surprise. "Gladys Gatsby?" she said. "This was *your* idea?"

"Uh . . ." Gladys rubbed her eyes, still blinded by the flash. Hamilton's letter was practically burning a hole through her backpack, and the last thing she wanted to do was get enmeshed in a long interview about bake sale planning. "Sort of," she said quickly. "I mean, I like to bake, so I was happy to jump in."

Elaine's camera was gone faster than seemed humanly possible, replaced by a small pad on which she scribbled furious notes. "So let me get this straight," she said. "You don't have time to join clubs like, say, *the newspaper* . . . but you *do* have time to bake hundreds of cookies for a team you're not actually on?"

Was it bad to help a team with their fund-raiser if you weren't a member? Gladys didn't think so, but figured it couldn't hurt to clarify. "I didn't do any of the actual baking," she said quickly. "I just sort of . . . supervised and consulted."

"But to be clear, you're *not* on the soccer team, right?" Elaine gave Gladys a cool stare. "Never mind, no need to answer. The roster's public information—I can always pop by the gym and check."

Now it really sounded like Elaine was trying to get Gladys into trouble. "Look," Gladys said, "I was just trying to do something nice for a friend. I mean, I'd be happy to help any club out with a bake sale if they asked me."

"Help a friend. How sweet." Elaine sneered like friendship was something she had stopped having time for in first grade. "Well, I've got everything I need for now. Thanks, Gladys. Very enlightening." With that, she flipped her pad shut and disappeared.

Fudge. Gladys had enough going on—she certainly

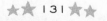

didn't need a vindictive middle-school reporter on her case, too.

She could see that the sale was going fine without her help, and although she was hungry enough to eat all the treats left on the table, she was even more eager to read her letter. She made a phone with her hand to signal Parm to call her later, then wiggled her way out of the crowd toward the exit.

Extra glad that she had ridden her bike that morning, Gladys pedaled the few blocks home as though that comet from the teachers' orientation shirts was on her tail.

The house was empty; both of her parents were at work, and Aunt Lydia must have been out shopping or something. Still, Gladys retreated to her bedroom and closed the door before taking the letter out of her backpack. She ripped into the envelope and pulled out the single typed sheet inside.

But as soon as she glimpsed the signature, she realized that she had been wrong. This letter wasn't from Hamilton at all.

Dear Gladys,

I've just discovered that this year you are taking French with my neighbor Lillian Goldstein. I've informed her that, based on my own interactions

*with you, she is very lucky to have you in her
class!*

*I hope that you'll excuse the cloak-and-dagger
maneuvers I have undertaken to get this letter
into your hands, but I imagine that as soon
as you saw the way I wrote your name on the
envelope, you understood my reasoning. I didn't
want to mention anything last year when you
were still in my class, for fear of making you feel
uncomfortable or exposed. But now that you're
not my student anymore, I figure that we can be
more honest with each other, peer-to-peer—or
perhaps I should say foodie-to-foodie?* ☺

   *In any case, I wanted to let you know that I
am extremely proud of your accomplishments
so far in the field of restaurant criticism and
that I am following your career with the greatest
interest. You cannot imagine the rush of pride I
feel, as your former teacher, every time I see your
byline appear in the* Standard.

   *I'm hoping to see many more mouthwatering
articles from you. I also wanted to say that if
you ever need an adult to talk to—discreetly,
of course—about your work, I would be happy*

to be of service. You can contact me anytime at the e-mail address or phone number below (or, if you prefer, reply by letter via our mutual amie, *Madame Goldstein).*

All my best,
Violetta Quincy

Gladys finished reading the letter, then reached for the torn envelope she had cast aside so quickly. *G. Gatsby,* it said in neat block letters. The abbreviated byline she used on her reviews for the *Standard.*

Really, it was wonderful to hear from her sixth-grade teacher. Ms. Quincy was, after all, the one who had encouraged her to be true to her passion and write about becoming a restaurant critic for the *New York Standard* essay contest. It was that essay that had somehow fallen into the hands of Fiona Inglethorpe and led to Gladys's first professional reviewing assignment.

Gladys had been pretty sure that Aunt Lydia and Mr. Eng were the only two adults in the world who knew about her secret job—but it seemed that her former teacher had figured it out as well. And it was so nice of Ms. Quincy to get in touch now and offer her support. She would definitely have to write back to her soon to thank her.

But despite the way the letter had buoyed her, Gladys couldn't help but feel a twinge of disappointment that it wasn't from Hamilton. She had started making excuses to herself for why he hadn't returned her call, but still, she wasn't ready to give up on him completely. She took down her copy of *Zombietown, U.S.A.,* went to the office, and dialed his number again. But, just like last time, a recording answered on the first ring.

It was a different recording from last time, though. "We're sorry," said a robotic voice, "but the voice-mail box of the person you are trying to reach is full."

How strange—had no one in Hamilton's family been checking the voice mail? If that was the case, then maybe Hamilton hadn't even gotten Gladys's original message.

She sighed. How to reach him, if not by phone? If Hamilton was on DumpChat, the local online instant-messaging service, she didn't know his username. And they hadn't exchanged e-mail addresses that summer, which Gladys was starting to see as a major oversight. She supposed that Charissa might have an e-mail address for the Herbertsons on file at her parents' camp office, but Gladys really didn't want to ask; Charissa was not a big fan of Hamilton, and his most recent display at school hadn't done him any favors with her.

Gladys picked absently at the silver "Finalist for Best Kids Author at the Kids Rock Awards!" sticker on the cover of Hamilton's book. Its corner lifted, revealing some tiny print that she had never noticed before.

It said *Visit www.ZombietownUSA.com for more info about the book and tween author sensation Hamilton Herbertson.*

Bingo!

A few moments later, Gladys had the website up on the computer; it featured the black cover of Hamilton's book, with the tagline "The literary phenomenon that's sweeping the nation!"

Gladys clicked on the book cover, and the main site came up; there were tabs labeled "About the Book" and "About the Author." Gladys clicked on the second one and was greeted with a black-and-white head-shot of Hamilton that took up half the screen. She had never really thought about it before, but in this picture, with his signature fedora angled jauntily, he actually looked sort of . . . cute.

Stop it, Gladys told herself. Hamilton Herbertson was many things—annoying, self-centered, clueless about basic social interactions—but "cute" was definitely not one of them. Just the same, Gladys didn't feel comfortable looking at his picture anymore, and quickly clicked back to the home page. There, she noticed another tab, "Contact," and clicked over to it.

Hey, readers—got a question for Hamilton? Send it in to us at ztown@futureflame.com.

Well, that was a start. Gladys clicked on the e-mail address, which automatically opened a DumpMail message, and started typing.

To Whom It May Concern,

I'm a friend of Hamilton's, and I'm trying to get ahold of him. Would you please ask him to e-mail me at ggatsby@dumpmail.com? It's important. Thank you very much.

Sincerely,
Gladys Gatsby

There, she thought as she sent the e-mail, *that should do it.*

She was about to log off and start on her homework when her DumpChat chime dinged.

rabbitboy: backyard plz

Today had been Sandy's gross-off at school— he probably wanted to celebrate his victory. Gladys wished she had thought to snag at least one brownie from the bake sale for him, but he'd just have to accept her empty-handed congratulations. She bounded down the stairs, outside, and across the yard—but the expression on Sandy's face when she reached the gap in the hedge stopped her in her tracks.

Chapter 15

DEATH BY DURIAN

"I LOST," SANDY SAID MISERABLY. "IT wasn't even close."

"What?" Gladys couldn't believe what she was hearing. "But that cheese—it was *so* disgusting! What could possibly have topped that?"

Sandy took a deep, shaky breath. His normally red cheeks weren't tearstained, but they were as pale as Gladys had ever seen them. "It was a fruit," he said. "Of all things, a *fruit*! On the outside, it looked kind of like a mutant pineapple, and on the inside it had these alien-like pods of yellow flesh. But ugh, you could smell it before Jonah even cut into it. Like a combination of raw onions and metal and . . . I don't know, just rot."

"A durian," Gladys said quietly.

"Wait—you knew this fruit existed?"

Sandy glared at Gladys accusingly, as if she had been withholding important information from him on purpose.

"Well, yeah," Gladys said. "Some people like it; some people despise it. I've always been curious to try it, actually, but I have no idea where to find it in America. It's from Southeast Asia."

"Chinatown, in the city," Sandy said with a sigh. "Jonah got his parents to take him over the weekend; he said he spent hours asking around at different fruit stands until he found one. And all I did was walk to Mr. Eng's and grab the first thing I tried. I deserved to lose."

"Don't say that!" Gladys cried. "That Limburger cheese was a great choice! I mean, the other kids must have at least agreed that it was pretty gross, right?"

"They did at first," Sandy said. "I even offered some to the others to try, and a few did. But then Jonah took out his fruit, and *everything* about it was disgusting. The texture was goopy and slimy. And the flavor . . . well, it was sort of sweet at first—just enough to trick you into trying another bite—but then the true, horrible taste came out. And *that* taste stayed in your mouth for hours, no matter what else you ate, even more Limburger cheese." Sandy sighed again. "Jonah won fair and square."

Gladys hated to admit it, but it sounded like Sandy was right.

"Okay, so maybe this round went to Jonah," she said, "but he's got to give you another chance! When's the rematch? I know we can find you something even better than a durian."

She expected Sandy to perk up at this, but like the taste of durian that had apparently lingered in his mouth all day, his glum demeanor stuck around. "I dunno, Gatsby. Maybe I should just know when I'm beaten and accept it."

Gladys had never heard Sandy sound so pessimistic—it was almost like he had temporarily swapped personalities with Parm. "No *way*," she said. "This is not the Sandy Anderson I know. You can win this thing! You've just got to . . . you know, believe in yourself and stuff!"

Finally, a small grin cracked Sandy's face. "Wow, Gatsby. That's some motivational speech."

"Sorry." Gladys shook her head. This was why she loved writing—you could take hours to come up with the perfect phrase if you needed to. Face-to-face communication was so much harder.

"Nah, it's okay. I'm glad you believe in me." Sandy reached a fist through the gap in the hedge, and Gladys bumped it. "Jonah did say he'd take on any fool who was still willing to challenge him, but of course, no one spoke up. Maybe, though . . . if I can find something *really* amazingly disgusting . . ."

"You can!" Gladys cried. "I know you can. We'll do it

together. I'm planning to head into the city this week-end to visit my first restaurant for the new reviews—you can come and we'll start looking."

But Sandy shook his head. "Can't do this week-end—yoga retreat with Mom upstate. She's teaching, and they're letting her bring me for free. I'll do my own sleuthing there, but the whole menu's vegan, so my hopes aren't high."

"Oh. Okay." Gladys wondered what Sandy would do during the retreat—would he take his mom's classes? Would that be weird for him? Gladys had gone to work with her dad a couple of times in the past year, though the hours she'd spent in his accounting meetings had been some of the most boring of her life. Yoga, at least, sounded more interesting.

"So let me know the next time you're heading into the city, and hopefully I can come," Sandy said.

Gladys nodded. "And I'll keep my eyes . . . and nose . . . open in the meantime."

When Parm called her that night, Gladys found even more evidence for her personality-swapping theory: Parm's voice was more upbeat than Gladys had ever heard it. "We sold every last treat!" she cried. "By the end, I'd raised the prices on the barfi to two bucks apiece, and even then, kids were fighting over them. We made six hundred dollars—that's more than one-third of our fund-raising goal for the trip!"

"That's great!" Gladys said.

"Coach was so happy," Parm continued, "and now I'm pretty much the most popular girl on the team. *Not* that popularity is important to me *at all*," she added quickly. "Like I tell Charissa over and over, being popular is stupid. But money is good! We're just a couple more bake sales away from going to Pennsylvania!"

Gladys smiled. "I'm so glad it all worked out."

"We couldn't have done it without you, obviously," Parm said. "And the rest of the team is really grateful, too. They were talking about making you an honorary member."

"Honorary member?" Gladys smiled, imagining the look on Elaine de la Vega's face if she actually saw Gladys's name listed on the soccer team roster after all.

"Well, if you ever want to come work out with us one day after school or something, you'd be welcome," Parm said.

Gladys laughed then, trying to imagine herself dribbling or passing a soccer ball. "I think I'll stick to dribbling icing on scones and passing the salt at the dinner table—but thanks."

"Well, anyway, I owe you big. Is there something I can do to help you with"—here, Parm lowered her voice—"you know, your job?"

Gladys nudged the office door shut with her foot, then lowered her own voice for good measure. "Well," she said, "you could come with me and my aunt on one of our restaurant research trips and order extra food. Asking for half the stuff on the menu will look less weird with three people eating instead of two, you know?"

"Done—as long as you don't make me *eat* the stuff I order," Parm said. "Just let me know when you need me, and as long as I don't have practice, I'll be there."

After she got off the phone, Gladys crossed the hallway and tapped on the guest room door. When Aunt Lydia opened it, Gladys could tell she was in a better mood than the night before, since she was dressed for bed in silk mint-green pajamas rather than her old sweats.

Gladys sat on the edge of her aunt's bed. "So, how did it go at Mr. Eng's today?" she asked. They hadn't been able to discuss things in front of Gladys's parents at dinner.

"I could hardly believe it," Aunt Lydia said. "He didn't want to fire me at all! Instead, he wants to send me to some foodie trade shows to scout out new products for the store."

As tired as Gladys was of keeping secrets, she didn't think it would be right to let on that the whole send-Aunt-Lydia-to-conventions plan had been her idea. So instead, she simply smiled and said, "That's great, Aunt Lydia!"

"The first one is a dried-meats convention this

Saturday in the city," Aunt Lydia said. "Mr. Eng even suggested it might be fun for you to tag along—you know, sort of as my assistant."

Gladys grinned, and not just because that had also been her idea. A dried-meats convention sounded like the perfect place to hunt for something stomach-turning for Sandy. Maybe there would even be actual dried stomach!

"I'd love to," Gladys said. "And can we visit the Sal-vadoran restaurant in Queens after?"

"Absolutely," Aunt Lydia said. "I can call tomor-row and make us a reservation—under my name, of course."

"Make it for three," Gladys said. "I'm going to see if Charissa can join us—I think she'd be helpful."

Aunt Lydia nodded, and after they had exchanged good night *bisoux* on each cheek, Gladys headed for her own bedroom.

Parm's bake sale had been a success, she had found an e-mail address for Hamilton, she and Sandy had a plan for his next battle, and her first reviewing outing was scheduled. Plus, the French Club would be meeting tomorrow.

Gladys fell asleep feeling like maybe she was finally starting to get the hang of life in middle school.

Chapter 16

BAKE SALE FAIRY GODMOTHER?

GLADYS'S IMPRESSION THAT HER LIFE was under control lasted all of twelve hours.

Students were posted at either side of the school's main entrance the next morning, reaching into boxes to hand something to each kid who went through the doors. "Get your paper!" one of them shouted as Gladys approached. "Special back-to-school edition of the *DTMS Telegraph*!"

Although Gladys still had absolutely no desire to join the school paper, she couldn't help but feel a little curious about how Elaine's pet project would read. Would its features be up to *New York Standard* level? Or more along the lines of stories found in the typo-ridden *Dumpsford Township Intelligencer*?

Whatever the quality, this first issue of the school year looked short: just the front and back of one legal-sized sheet of paper, folded in half. Gladys accepted her copy from the paperboy to her right, unfolded it—and froze.

There was one picture on the front page of the paper, and it was of her.

Someone bumped into her from behind. "Hey!" a kid farther back shouted. "Who's holding up the line?"

"It's her!" another voice shouted. "The girl in the paper!"

Gladys finally forced herself to move forward, faster and faster until she was practically running down the hallway. She spotted a bathroom and ducked inside, then locked herself in the first empty stall. Finally, heart pounding more from nerves than from her sprint, she opened the newspaper sheet again.

The picture wasn't very flattering—it had been taken from an odd angle, and Gladys was cringing away rather than looking at the camera. Still, she noticed Owen and Charissa and the table of treats from the bake sale in the background.

But much worse than the picture was the article that went along with it.

GLADYS GATSBY:
Bake Sale Fairy Godmother or Blatant Rule-Breaker?

Special Investigative Report
by Editor in Chief Elaine de la Vega

Seventh-grader Gladys Gatsby is new to DTMS, but that doesn't mean that she's eager to learn our school's rules.

At yesterday's well-attended soccer team bake sale (see "Super-Successful Bake Sale Breaks School Records" by Elaine de la Vega, pg. 2), Ms. Gatsby stood front and center. One would assume that this sale was organized by members of the soccer team. But when this reporter spoke to seventh-grade player Parminder Singh and asked what the team's secret ingredient was, she said, "Talk to . . . Gladys Gatsby."

Ms. Gatsby herself admitted that she had designed treats for the sale and supervised the baking, and she did not appear at all apologetic. Instead, she said that she would "help any club out with a bake sale if they asked me"—in short, guaranteeing that she plans to keep up with this unethical practice.

These shenanigans appear to be nothing new for Ms. Gatsby, who also had a record of dodgy behavior at East Dumpsford Elementary School last year. "She totally started a food fight in the cafeteria," says ex-classmate Mira Winters. "Or, at least, she was involved. I saw her throw a sandwich, but she never got in trouble."

Perhaps this pattern of escaping punishments in the past has led Ms. Gatsby to believe that she will be invincible at DTMS. But if she's asked to "consult" on another soccer team bake sale, this reporter suggests that Ms. Gatsby design a cookie in the shape of a "red card."

Gladys stared at the article in disbelief. The homeroom bell rang, but she didn't move—might as well add a tardy to her growing list of "crimes."

She had only wanted to help Parm—okay, and maybe get in a little extra kitchen time. She had really thought that the only rule she was breaking was her parents' dumb one about only cooking once a week. But now . . .

Gladys pictured the boxes full of newspapers at the school entrance. How long before a copy made its way onto the desk of Parm's soccer coach, or Dr. Sloane? What if they made Parm's team return all the money they raised? Gladys's stomach filled with liquid dread. More than any potential embarrassment for herself, she worried over what Elaine's "investigative report" could mean for her friend.

Well, about that, at least, she could try to do something. If she explained herself to the authorities, and swore that it was her mistake alone, she might be able to stop the team from suffering any consequences. Gladys pushed open the stall door and hurried out of the bathroom.

A sour-faced aide stood only a few feet away. "Hall pass?"

"I don't have one," Gladys said.

"Then you'll be going straight to the principal's office, young lady."

"Great," Gladys muttered. "I was heading there anyway."

The aide stuck to her side and kept a beady eye on her as they progressed down the hallway and turned the corner to the office. Gladys wondered if she, too, had read the article in the paper or just treated all passless students like juvenile delinquents.

The secretary asked Gladys to have a seat and wait since the principal was in with another student. Gladys wondered who had managed to get into trouble even before she had that morning. It didn't take long for her to find out—Dr. Sloane's raised voice carried right through her closed door.

"This is completely unacceptable!" she bellowed. "Your adviser and I had both approved the other version. Did you really think we wouldn't notice that you switched the files?"

The student's response was too muffled for Gladys to hear.

"Switched by accident before you hit 'Print'? That's quite a story, Elaine—possibly almost as libelous as the one you chose to publish about a fellow student."

Gladys's heart gave a tiny jolt of surprise. Was Dr. Sloane talking about the newspaper? She listened more closely.

"It was just . . . an early draft . . . never meant to publish . . ." Elaine's voice, still quiet, seemed to be broken up by sobs, and when Dr. Sloane responded, her voice sounded a bit kinder.

"All right, Elaine. I understand that you're under a lot of pressure with such a small newspaper staff," she said. "Maybe you really never meant for that article to see the light of day. But still, we can't have such sloppy work. You'll need to retract that story and issue a correction in your next issue. And I'd also like for you to apologize to Ms. Gatsby."

A moment later, the intercom on the secretary's desk buzzed. "Kate, would you call down to Gladys Gatsby's homeroom and have her sent to the office, please?"

The secretary looked down at the intercom, then up at Gladys. "Um, she's already here, Dr. Sloane. Waiting to see you."

"She is? Well . . . send her in then, please."

Gladys shot to her feet, though her first instinct

was to bolt for the exit. The last person she wanted to face this morning was Elaine—even a weepy Elaine.

Come on now, she told herself. Parm didn't shy away from her opponents on the soccer field; Sandy was gearing up for a *third* gross foods match with Jonah even though he'd lost the first two. And Charissa wasn't afraid of anybody. Couldn't Gladys draw on a little bit of their courage, too?

She turned to the principal's door, squared her shoulders, and marched in.

Elaine was on her feet, her fierce demeanor not quite able to make up for her blotchy face.

"Ah, Gladys—I see that you've already seen the newspaper," Dr. Sloane said.

Gladys realized that her copy of the paper was still clutched in her left hand. She let her grip relax and laid the copy down on the principal's desk. Then she cleared her throat and looked straight at Dr. Sloane, ignoring Elaine as best she could. "I just wanted to say, Dr. Sloane, that helping the soccer team with their bake sale was my idea, and mine alone. If I'd realized that it was against the rules, I never would have offered, and I really hope that you won't penalize them for my mistake."

Dr. Sloane shook her head. "It's not against any rule, Gladys; Elaine's article was quite exaggerated. Now, if you'd done all the work for them and let them take the credit, that would be a problem, but if you just offered help of your own free will, no one's going to fault you for that."

Gladys let out a huge sigh of relief. Dr. Sloane, though, wasn't finished. "Of course, in the future I hope that you'll consider actually joining some clubs here rather than simply helping with fund-raising without gaining the benefits of membership. Does that sound fair?"

Membership in a bunch of clubs sounded more like a burden to Gladys than a benefit, but she nodded anyway.

"And as for the article . . ." Dr. Sloane continued. "Elaine tells me that it was something she drafted for her own amusement, and that she never meant to publish it for a wide readership. Elaine, do you have something that you'd like to add?"

Dr. Sloane looked pointedly at Elaine, whose blood-shot gaze turned upon Gladys. "I'm sorry that I sent the wrong file to the printer yesterday," Elaine said robotically. "I'll be more careful in the future."

Wrong file, my foot, Gladys thought. Thanks to her work with the *Standard,* she knew how much time and effort went into newspaper layout every day; it really wasn't possible to accidentally stick in a major story and picture.

Thinking about the *Standard,* though, reminded Gladys that she had much bigger secrets to protect than the fact that she'd helped out with a middle-school bake sale. If she could get "Investigative Reporter" Elaine de la Vega on her good side—or, at least, off her bad side—she should probably do it.

"I accept your apology," she said through gritted teeth.

"Very good," Dr. Sloane said. "I'm glad to see you girls are both being mature about this. Now, Gladys, Elaine assures me she'll print a retraction in the paper's next issue, so I believe we're finished here. You can both go back to class."

Gladys shot out the door before Elaine had even reached for the strap of her messenger bag. Soon enough, she was lost in the crowd of students making their way to first period, and she didn't look back. In fact, she was wondering how hard it would be to avoid coming face-to-face with Elaine de la Vega ever again.

Chapter 17

BAKED GOODS AND BRAINS

"SO IS IT REALLY TRUE?"

Joanna Rodriguez, one of Gladys's old classmates from East Dumpsford Elementary, was waiting for her in first-period science. She had a copy of the newspaper in her hand.

Great. Dr. Sloane may have made Elaine promise to print a retraction, but until then, the story was still out there for everyone to read.

"What, that I'm a giant rule-breaker?" Gladys couldn't help but snarl.

Joanna's big brown eyes widened. "What? No, not that part. The part where it says you designed the whole bake sale—and that you'd be willing to help other clubs with theirs."

"Oh." Gladys felt sheepish now for having snapped at her. "Uh, sure. Why?"

The bell rang just then, and their teacher barked at Joanna to take her seat. She did, but the moment his back was turned, a tiny folded-up note landed on Gladys's desk.

She snatched it up and shoved it into her pocket, caution winning out over curiosity—she'd already had enough brushes with serious trouble that morning.

When class ended, Gladys took the note with her and read it on the way to gym: *I'm in Art Club, and we'd love to have you help us plan our fund-raiser! We meet on Fridays. Come this week!—JoRo*

An invitation to join another club? That was the last thing Gladys had expected to result from this debacle. But as it turned out, Joanna's invitation was only the first of many.

In the gym locker room, two girls Gladys had never talked to before asked if she had ever thought about running cross-country. Gladys was sure they must be pranking her, until one mentioned that the team hoped to raise money with a bake sale.

Then, at lunchtime, Gladys didn't even need to make a special effort to avoid Elaine de la Vega, because a small group was waiting for her at her regular lunch table. Charissa's friend Rolanda was one of them, and she spoke first.

"Hey, Gladys—how are you?" She shot Gladys a gleaming-toothed grin and tossed her tiny braids over her shoulder. "So, I'm in Drama Club now, and I was wondering if you might consider trying out for the fall musical. We'd *really* love to have you in the cast! And to raise money for new costumes, we were thinking of holding a bake—"

"Hey, Gladys, I'm Jason Mitty." Before Rolanda could finish, a boy pushed past her, his hand outstretched. "Newly elected president of the Chess Club. Have you ever played?"

Gladys shook her head.

"Well, no worries—we can teach you! Beginners are always welcome. And hey, let me get your opinion on something: chess-piece candies. How hard would they be to make? Because we were thinking, for our bake sale—"

At this, a lanky, freckled girl stepped in front of him. "Forget all of them," she insisted. "I'm Shayla Brown. Your buddy Charissa is already a Mathlete—why don't you join us, too? Unlike these jokers, we want you for your brain, not just your baking expertise. Although, I've got to say, some sort of brain-shaped baked good *would* be pretty fitting for our sale . . ."

Gladys was starting to feel smothered by all the attention—but at the same time, she couldn't help but feel a tiny bit triumphant. Elaine had clearly meant to sabotage her reputation with that article, but it turned out she had advertised Gladys's baking skills much more effectively than Gladys could have done on her own. And with the cooking restrictions still firmly in place at her house, these clubs might be her only chance to get back into the kitchen regularly!

"Okay," she told the kids clustered around her. "I'll join."

"Wait—which one?" Rolanda asked. "Which club do you pick?"

"I pick all of them," Gladys said simply.

"But . . ." Shayla gaped at her like a bigmouthed fish. "But Mathletes is a big commitment!"

"Yeah, and so is Chess Club!" Jason said. "We meet once a week after school, and then there are tournaments—"

"Shh!" Rolanda hissed at them both. "If Gladys says she wants to join all of our clubs, then she can join them. She obviously knows how much she can handle." She shot Gladys another grin. "Drama meets after school today in the auditorium. We'll see you at two-thirty."

"Chess Club's next meeting is Thursday in the music annex," Jason said.

"And Mathletes meets tomorrow in Mrs. Vicole's classroom," Shayla said. "See you then?"

"Sure," Gladys said, but as the three club leaders walked away, she felt a twinge of apprehension. In less than five minutes, she'd somehow managed to commit herself to an extracurricular agenda that rivaled Charissa's. Hadn't she told her friend that was a bad idea?

When Gladys saw Charissa again in French that

afternoon, she started to doubt her decision even more. Charissa was already looking fried—and not in a crispy, appealing way. There were bags under her eyes, her normally glowing skin was sallow, and her knuckles were white as she clutched a small notebook, muttering about that evening's schedule. "After the bell, Student Leadership Council. If that lets out early, switch to French Club."

French Club! Gladys knew she had forgotten something important when she'd committed to going to Drama Club that afternoon. She groaned. She had told Rolanda she would be there; she supposed she'd just have to pick up with French Club next week.

Charissa, meanwhile, was still talking to herself. "Pickup at four and straight on to ballet. Dinner at six. Homework at seven. Science quiz tomorrow—don't forget to study . . ."

Gladys hated to interrupt, but back at camp, Charissa had made Gladys promise to let her know when her next restaurant-reviewing trip was scheduled. "Hey, Charissa," she whispered, "want to come with me on Saturday to a Salvadoran restaurant in Queens?"

Charissa paused in her schedule recitation and turned to Gladys, her weary eyes brightening momentarily. "Yeah!" she said. "Awesome! Is Parm coming, too?"

"Oh—um, no," Gladys said. "It'll just be you, me, and Aunt Lydia."

"Oh. Okay."

Was Gladys imagining it, or did Charissa sound a little sad about that?

"Just let me know what time I need to be ready," she said, "and I'll put it in my planner." She flipped open her small notebook, and Gladys saw an elaborate, color-coded schedule. "I'll label it in green—that's the color I reserve for fun." At first glance, Gladys didn't notice any other "fun" slots reserved for the month of September.

After class—and after apologizing to Madame Goldstein—Gladys proceeded to the Drama Club meeting as promised. There she learned, thankfully, that you could be a member without having to perform onstage, and she quickly signed up to paint scenery instead. Although she wasn't really confident that her painting skills were any better than her acting ones, she figured that job held less potential for public humiliation. And who knew—maybe she would even pick up some skills at an Art Club meeting that would help her.

Once the crew sign-ups were done and the audition schedule was announced, the Drama Club adviser, Mr. Hollon, asked everybody to huddle up onstage so they could brainstorm ideas for their fund-raiser bake sale the next week. As Gladys climbed the stage steps, she couldn't help but think back to the last time she'd stood up there, after Hamilton's presentation. She wondered whether he had gotten her e-mail yet.

The brainstorming part of the meeting was by far the most fun for Gladys; it seemed that everyone had read the article in the *Telegraph,* and they automatically looked to her for guidance. In the end, they took her suggestion of baking a variation on black-and-white iced cookies featuring the traditional comedy and tragedy masks of Greek drama. Icing the cookies properly would take some work, but when Gladys passed a sign-up sheet around, almost twenty kids volunteered to meet her the next Monday evening at Rolanda's house to bake.

That night at the dinner table, Gladys's parents were thrilled to hear that she had joined some new clubs—though she conveniently left out the detail that she'd be running all their bake sales.

"Well, I have some good news, too," her mom announced as she served herself more of the pasta bolognaise Aunt Lydia had prepared. "I finally got ahold of the owner of the Pathetti's Pies property, and he's going to give me the listing."

"That's great!" Gladys's dad crowed, and Aunt Lydia and Gladys added their congratulations, too.

"Yes, well, don't get too excited yet," her mom said. "I don't think it's going to be easy to find a new tenant."

Gladys's dad reached for the cheese. "Why not?"

"The interior needs a lot of work," her mom said.

"New paint job, new light fixtures, and so on, but Bob doesn't want to take care of any of those details. Whoever leases the space is going to need to do a lot of work on their own." She sighed.

"At least you got the listing, Jen," Aunt Lydia piped up. "That's something!"

"Thanks," her mom said. "Well, if you hear any customers at Mr. Eng's talking about wanting to lease a dilapidated former pizzeria, make sure you give them my card." She laughed. "And you too, Gladys—keep your ears open at all those club meetings. You never know where a lead might come from!"

Gladys had reserved the next day with her parents for kitchen access, and she was planning, at long last, to try her hand at some Salvadoran specialties. After dinner, she made some preparations, like setting a pot of beans out on the counter with water to soak and retrieving a shoulder of pork from the freezer to thaw overnight. Before she left for school the next morning, she would set it up in the slow cooker with liquid and spices so that when she got home, she'd have pulled pork ready to stuff into her pupusa dough.

Finally, before she went to bed, Gladys checked her e-mail, but there was no response yet from Hamilton. *Maybe my note hasn't been forwarded to him yet,* she told herself, and attempted to put it out of her mind. Instead, she DumpChatted with Sandy and asked if he and his mom would like to come over for pupusas the following night. At first, Sandy was excited because the word *pupusa*—like *barfi*—sounded a little disgusting in English. But even when Gladys told him it was just a stuffed cornmeal pancake, he agreed to come try it.

Chapter 18

PUPUSA PERFECTION

GLADYS WAS LUCKY THAT MRS. ANDERSON had volunteered to bring dessert, because she arrived home the next day much later than she'd anticipated. Despite having Charissa in her corner, getting the Mathletes to settle on a bake sale concept had been much harder than it had been with the Drama Club.

Finally, after learning that Shayla's parents had just bought a new deep fryer, Gladys had had an idea. In her research about Cuban food for her upcoming review, she'd been looking at recipes for buñuelos, a sort of doughnut made with yucca flour and licorice-y anise flavoring. In Cuba, they were made twisted into figure eights, but why couldn't they be shaped like any number? The idea of number-shaped doughnuts was a hit, and Shayla promised that everyone could come to her house to make them once a bake sale date had been secured.

Despite her late start on the Salvadoran dinner at home, Gladys's pupusas came out well. The pancakes proved harder to stuff with meat, beans, and cheese than she'd expected, and several of them developed leaky cracks as she griddled them. But she was able to cover up those imperfections with curtido—a slightly fermented cabbage-and-carrot condiment that was traditionally eaten with pupusas in El Salvador—and nobody at the table seemed to notice.

"Really wonderful dinner, Gladys," Mrs. Anderson said after polishing off her third pupusa. "But I have to ask, what brought this recipe to your attention? Do you subscribe to an international cooking newsletter? If so, I'd love the link."

Gladys blinked nervously. Only Sandy and Aunt Lydia knew the true reason for Gladys's sudden interest in Salvadoran cooking—and for now, she wanted to keep it that way.

"Well, we'll be doing the history of the Americas in seventh grade this year," she said, thinking fast, "so I thought it would be cool to try cuisines from some other countries." And really, there was nothing false about that—Gladys was always happy to learn about new cuisines.

Mrs. Anderson, though, seemed impressed. "How

conscientious of you! Sandy could stand to take a page out of your book." She beamed at Gladys, then gave Sandy a gentle nudge. He didn't look up from his plate, where he was busy arranging his curtido into a wild multicolored mop of hair on top of his round white pupusa. The pancake already had eye-holes that were oozing refried beans, and a jack-o'-lantern grin.

Mrs. Anderson nudged him again, and this time his head snapped up.

"Whuh?" he said. "Time for dessert?"

Gladys tried to hold in her giggles.

Sandy's mom sighed, but a minute later she brought out the plate of pumpkin bars she had baked that day. Gladys grabbed one. She definitely needed more sustenance if she was going to make it through the rest of her busy week.

By the time Gladys, Aunt Lydia, and Charissa headed into the city on the train that Saturday, Gladys was ready for a break. After school on Thursday, Jason Mitty had insisted on cramming chess rules into her already overstuffed brain, and she'd spent Friday afternoon trying—and failing—to explain to the Art Club why recreating Rodin's sculpture *The Thinker* out of marzipan was not the best idea for their bake sale. Then she had stayed up late helping her aunt prepare for her first trade show.

Charissa was exhausted as well from her own extracurricular commitments, so it was left to Aunt Lydia to rally the troops. "Dried meats! In styles from all around the world!" she cried, waving a catalog in the girls' faces. "Oh, I hardly know which booth to head to first. Montana-made elk jerky? Chinese-inspired yak-meat floss? Look, there'll even be horse-meat snack bites 'in the traditional Mongolian style'!"

"Horse?" Charissa's half-closed, violet-shaded eyes snapped open, and she grabbed the catalog. "Oh, *gross*! I *ride* horses every Thursday!" She turned to Gladys, a pleading look in her eye. "Let's steer clear of that booth, okay?"

"Sure," Gladys said, but when her friend's eyelids closed again, Gladys whispered to her aunt, "Try to grab me a few of those horse-meat bites for Sandy, okay?"

Aunt Lydia winked. "I'll do my best."

The trade show was set up on the floor of a convention center, a cavernous indoor space filled with booths advertising their wares. Colorful banners flew high above tables, some of them showing pictures of the different animals that supplied their meats. Gladys, Charissa, and Lydia all paused to take in the sheer amount of colors, scents, and sounds that surrounded them. Then Aunt Lydia busted out the spreadsheet she and Gladys had made the night before, and they started off down one of the aisles.

First they were beckoned by vendors waving Australian flags and offered samples of dried emu, camel, and kangaroo. Next they sampled biltong (a South African–style jerky), which came in slabs, chunks, chips, and, Gladys's favorite, snappy sausage-like sticks called droëwors. In addition to beef, the biltong vendors offered a number of antelope meats, such as kudu and springbok, as well as ostrich (which tasted a lot like emu). In the Asian-inspired meat section, they tried yak meat that had been sweetened and processed to a feathery, almost cotton-candy-like consistency, and Charissa turned her back while Aunt Lydia sampled horse-meat bites.

Gladys was most intrigued by the vendors who raised animals from South America—llamas and alpacas—and offered up dried meats from both to try. A handout from one of these vendors taught her that the English word *jerky* actually came from the Quechua word *ch'arki,* which meant "dried, salted meat."

They finished up their tour of the convention center at a booth of vendors from Montana, who offered bison, elk, smoked duck breast, wild boar, and even alligator jerky.

Gladys had been careful only to take a nibble here and there since she wanted to save space in her stomach for the Salvadoran restaurant. Aunt Lydia and Charissa, however, hadn't bothered to hold back, and spent most of the long subway ride to Queens discussing their favorites and trying to decide which products might sell at Mr. Eng's.

"I'll definitely buy a lot of those kudu sticks if he starts carrying them," Charissa promised. "That would be a great protein snack for dance or cheerleading competitions."

Three cheers for dried kudu! Gladys thought.

In the end, Aunt Lydia narrowed her list down to seven candidates, which she would discuss further with Mr. Eng. "I'm not sure how many new products he wants to carry this fall," she said, "but that's why I picked up extra samples." Gladys had also made sure to grab some kangaroo and alligator samples for Sandy.

They got off the subway in Queens and reached the Salvadoran restaurant, Pupuseria El Gran Sabor, in time for a late lunch. As soon as Gladys walked in and heard the upbeat cumbia music playing, she felt her tired self perk up. It had been over a month since she'd reviewed a restaurant, and she was excited to taste what this one had to offer.

Soon enough, their table was weighted down with almost every specialty on the restaurant's short menu. Gladys was glad she'd made pupusas at home, because now she was really able to appreciate how perfectly formed and expertly cooked these ones were. Among the three of them, they were able to order and try every variety the restaurant offered, including one pupusa stuffed with a squash-like vegetable called chayote and another filled with nutty-tasting green flower buds called loroco. There were a few intriguing side dishes, too, like starchy fried yucca cubes and a beautifully seasoned rice-and-bean mixture called casamiento. And the drink choices were fascinating—fresh fruit juices in tropical flavors like papaya, guanabana, and marañon (which the menu described as "the fruit of the cashew plant").

By the time Aunt Lydia paid their bill—in cash—and tucked the receipt carefully into her purse for reimbursement, Gladys's stomach was nearly bursting and her reviewing notebook was full of notes about the unique cuisine of Central America's smallest country.

"That was really fun," Charissa said on the train back to East Dumpsford. "I wish I could come and help with all your assignments, but soon my weekends are really gonna start filling up. I've got a horseback competition next weekend, and my fall gymnastics showcase is the weekend after that . . ."

"No worries," Gladys said. "Sandy and Parm want to help out, too, so I'll let one of them come along on each of my next trips."

Charissa's brow furrowed. "Do you think Parm will actually eat? We have lunch together, and she always brings the same two things."

"You and Parm sit together at lunch?" For some reason, this surprised Gladys; considering how many

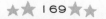

classes they had together, she would have thought Parm and Charissa might want a break from each other at lunchtime.

But Charissa didn't act like it was a big deal. "Yeah. Parm's cool. I mean, I'm not judging her for being picky or anything. It's kind of cute, how fussy she is."

Charissa not judging someone else's choices? That was new. Maybe Parm was turning out to be a good influence on her.

"So, you haven't mentioned Hamilton," Charissa prompted.

Gladys was taken aback by this turn in the conversation. "What do you mean?"

"I don't mean anything," Charissa said. "I just thought he was your friend, so maybe you'd invite him on one of your reviewing trips, too."

Maybe Gladys would have invited him . . . if he'd returned one of her messages. She had sent him a second e-mail through the Zombietown website that Thursday night, but as of this morning she still hadn't gotten a response.

"He lives somewhere nearby, right?" Charissa continued.

Gladys shrugged, trying to look nonchalant. "I have no idea where he lives."

Charissa blinked her wide, shadow-smeared eyes. "Ohmigosh. You *like* him!"

"What?" Clearly, Gladys's attempt at nonchalance had failed. "I don't *like* him! Ew."

Charissa raised an eyebrow, and Gladys wondered if maybe now she was protesting too much. Okay, on to plan B: role reversal. "Why are you bringing this up, anyway?" she asked. "Do *you* like someone or something?"

Gladys had only asked that to get the heat off herself; Charissa was so chatty that Gladys assumed she would spill the beans about any crush she had five minutes after she'd developed it. But to Gladys's surprise, Charissa's cheeks colored slightly, and she turned to stare out the train window. "Maybe," she said. Gladys waited another moment, but Charissa did not choose to elaborate.

Well, there's a first, Gladys thought. She was curious to know more, but she wasn't going to press if Charissa was willing to drop her line of inquiry about Hamilton. Still, Gladys wondered what it would be like if her friends started coupling up. Already since she had started middle school it had gotten hard to find time to spend together. If Charissa started going out with someone, would she have any time left in her color-coded schedule for Gladys?

Charissa's crazy schedule was still on Gladys's mind that night at home when she got started on her review for the *Standard*.

Some restaurants try to be everything to everyone, striving to appeal to the masses with long, varied menus. But others choose to limit their offerings to the dishes they know they can cook best. In the case of Pupuseria El Gran Sabor on Roosevelt Avenue in Queens, this second strategy pays off handsomely. The restaurant's small kitchen may only focus on a few items, but their perfect pupusas—complemented by a small selection of expertly cooked side dishes and unique juices—just about guarantee a delectable dining experience for anyone who pays them a visit . . .

Chapter 19

CULINARY SURPRISES

THE SKY WAS DARK THAT MONDAY evening when Gladys finally had a chance to ring Sandy's doorbell.

She had spent the afternoon at Rolanda's house working on the mask cookies with the Drama Club. Several of the other members actually had baking experience, which should have made the undertaking go more smoothly—and it did for a while, until everyone started belting out show tunes from *Phantom of the Opera*. Gladys left the house with both a splitting headache and an intense desire to see the chandelier in Rolanda's dining room come crashing down on every screeching, warbling Andrew Lloyd Webber fan there. In comparison, her street felt blissfully quiet.

Sandy answered his door dressed in

his white karate gi and greeted her by faking a kick in her direction. "What's up, Gatsby?" His bare foot stopped just short of nailing her in her cookie-dough-filled stomach.

Gladys groaned. "Way to welcome a girl into your house, Sandy." At least this was one friend who was in no danger of pairing up with a member of the opposite sex anytime soon. "I see that the yoga retreat didn't Zen you out too much."

"Zen is okay in small doses, but a kid has his limits," Sandy said, holding the screen door open for her. "How was your weekend? Mom's still upstairs, so you can talk as loud as you want."

Gladys followed him into the living room and spent a few minutes filling him in on the Salvadoran restaurant outing. She had spent Sunday carefully typing up her review (three and a half stars!) and had sent it to Fiona that evening; it would be published in Wednesday's Dining section.

"And I brought you these from the dried-meats trade show," Gladys said, reaching into her jacket pockets for the samples. "Alligator, kangaroo, and horse. What do you think?"

"Whoa." Sandy snatched up one of the horse-meat bites and examined the tiny lettering on its wrapper. "This is great. I'll give Jonah notice tomorrow that a new round of competition is coming his way!"

"Well, good luck," Gladys said. "Oh, and I wanted to

ask, are you free this Saturday? Do you want to come to a Cuban restaurant with me and my aunt?"

"Aggh!" Sandy karate-chopped at the air with one hand in frustration. "Saturday is family day at karate. Even my grandparents are coming to watch. Sorry, Gatsby."

"That's okay," Gladys said. She could always ask Parm to come that weekend. "But try to leave the following Saturday open if you can, okay? You, me, Aunt Lydia, and Peruvian food. Sound good?"

"Sounds excellent," Sandy said. "How should I prepare? Make spreadsheets? Look up recipes? Assemble a country map that highlights its regional specialties?"

"Those are all great ideas," Gladys said with a smile, "but you can leave the research to me. Just make sure you're hungry that day."

Sandy jumped into the air and landed in a wide-legged squat that made him look like a skinny blond sumo wrestler. "I won't eat for at least two hours beforehand," he said. "That should pretty much guarantee that I'll be rapturous."

Gladys didn't bother correcting him, even though she was pretty sure he actually meant *ravenous* (as in, very hungry). But who knew, maybe by then he'd actually be rapturous (as in, ecstatic), too—especially if the jerkies she'd brought him helped him claim the crown as Gross Foods King of St. Joseph's Academy.

At the Drama Club bake sale the next afternoon, the first customers Gladys saw were Parm and Charissa.

"Okay, let's get this party going!" Charissa cried. "I'll take ten of these awesome mask cookies. How much is that?"

"Twenty-five dollars," Gladys told her, since they'd priced the cookies at $2.50 each. Gladys started to gather up the cookies while, next to her, Rolanda opened up a cash box.

"Look at you two, working together," Charissa trilled. "You guys are friends now, and Parm and I are friends now . . . it's like we're one big, happy posse!"

From the way Rolanda wrinkled her nose, Gladys wasn't so sure that she agreed . . . and Parm looked a little skeptical, too.

"Parm, how many do you want?" Charissa asked.

"Well, as much as I'd like to support the Drama Club, I really don't want a cookie," Parm said. "No offense, but . . . it has a face on it! *Two* faces, actually." She shuddered.

"We're happy to take donations," Rolanda said sweetly. Parm scowled, but dug into her pocket.

"No, no, I've got it," Charissa insisted. "My treat." She dug out an extra five dollars and tossed it into the cash box.

It was one of the nicest things Gladys had ever seen

Charissa do for anybody; even Parm had to admit it. "Thanks, Charissa," she said.

Charissa beamed. "No problem." She gathered up the cookies that Gladys had put in a bag for her, then headed to French Club, which Gladys would once again be missing.

"I've got to get to practice," Parm said.

Gladys sent her off with a wave, but when she turned to assist her next customer, she found herself staring straight into the face of Elaine de la Vega.

Her mouth went dry. Elaine was grinning so widely that Gladys wondered if she was trying to imitate the exaggerated comedy mask on the cookies. In any case, it made for an eerie, unnatural look on the normally serious girl's face.

"Hello, Gladys," Elaine said. "Back at it with the baking, are we?"

Gladys swallowed hard. "That's right," she said, trying to sound confident. "Me and *my fellow Drama Club members* worked hard on these cookies. How many would you like?"

Elaine waved a hand in the air, as though cookies— like friends—were for children. "I'm just here to observe," she said. "You know, sniff out new leads. Our first full-length issue of the *Telegraph* will come out just after Halloween. With that retraction Sloane insisted on."

"Uh, that's great," Gladys said. Why was Elaine telling her this?

"So there's plenty of time for new stories to be written, and new photos to be taken. Do you know what I mean?"

The *Telegraph* editor's voice was almost chipper, but Gladys knew what was going on. Elaine was making a threat: telling Gladys that, despite the planned retraction, she was still keeping an eye on her. Between that and the girl's freaky grin, Gladys felt like someone had just released an ice cube into her bloodstream.

She wasn't going to give Elaine the satisfaction of showing that she was intimidated, though. "I have no idea what you mean," she said coolly. "And also, you're holding up the line. Paying customers have priority here—this is a *fund-raiser.*"

Elaine scowled, but moved away. Gladys let out a sigh of relief.

Pretty soon, cookies were flying off the table, and students who had bought just one were coming back for seconds and thirds. In the end, the Drama Club raked in over three hundred dollars, exceeding their goal for expanding the costume budget. When Rolanda announced the total, Gladys found herself getting more high fives than she'd ever gotten before. A pleasantly warm and fuzzy feeling was starting to spread through her usually nervous stomach. It stopped abruptly, though, when the group burst into song with a celebratory rendition of "The Music of the Night."

Between club meetings, schoolwork, and experimenting with a few Cuban recipes, the rest of the week flew by for Gladys. It wasn't until she was on the train beside Parm and Aunt Lydia on Saturday that it occurred to her she still hadn't heard from Hamilton.

Now she was starting to get nervous. Was he all right? Gladys thought back to their evening at the Kids Rock Awards—and how depressed he had been over his distant relationship with his parents. Plus, she knew he didn't have a lot of close friends. She really wished he would get in touch, if only to let her know that he was alive and well.

"Something on your mind?" Parm asked. "You seem a little . . . distracted."

Gladys shook her head. "It's nothing." She should be taking advantage of this rare one-on-one time with Parm, not wasting her energy wondering about Hamilton. He was probably fine—too busy attending literary parties to bother writing her back.

Parm now stared at Aunt Lydia as she flipped through a different trade show catalog, this one featuring olive oils from all over the Mediterranean. "Does she really have to go try a whole bunch of new foods every week?" she whispered to Gladys. "That's, like, my nightmare job."

The statement didn't surprise Gladys—Parm was by far her most finicky friend—but there was something about the way she said it that sounded strange to Gladys's ear. It took her a moment to figure out what, exactly, had struck her.

"The way you just said *like* . . ." Gladys said. "It didn't sound like you. It kind of sounded like . . . Charissa."

Parm's eyes widened. "Oh, no—don't tell me her speech patterns are rubbing off on me now!" She groaned. "I guess that's what happens when you have almost every class together."

"She told me you guys sit together at lunch, too," Gladys said with a smile.

Now Parm looked even more embarrassed. "We sit at a big table with a lot of other people."

"Hey, there's nothing wrong with changing your mind about someone," Gladys told her. "I've done it lots of times. And Charissa's really changed since last year, too."

"I guess she has," Parm said. "She's more studious than I would have thought. And it was great of her to support both of the bake sales like that. But that doesn't mean I want us to be besties."

"You can be friends without being best friends," Gladys said.

"Yeah, that's true. Well, then, I guess Charissa

Bentley is my friend. *Wow,* there's a sentence I never thought I'd say."

Gladys smiled again.

At the olive oil trade show, they wandered the aisles with Aunt Lydia, Parm refusing all samples as she filled Gladys in on her first couple of soccer matches. Then, in the afternoon, the three of them headed out for their late lunch at Café Havana in Queens.

Gladys's first impression of the restaurant was not very strong; its interior was a bit dusty and poorly lit, and the television in the corner blasting the Yankees game didn't add much to the ambience. But by the time she'd finished her meal, she had a much better feeling about the place. The tantalizing flavors of garlic, lime, and cumin infused many of the dishes she was served, and Gladys especially enjoyed her ropa vieja (a slow-simmered beef dish), fried sweet plantains, and buñuelo fritters, which she had not yet had a chance to make with the Mathletes. She felt slightly embarrassed when Parm pulled out a container of cereal she had brought from home. But Parm had done her duty of ordering extra dishes, and made a nice show of poking at her Cubano sandwich until Gladys had a chance to swoop in and try a few bites.

As they rode back to East Dumpsford on the train, Parm dozed off and Gladys drafted the opening lines for the second article in her series.

In life and in restaurants, first impressions rarely tell the whole story. The atmosphere at Café Havana may leave a lot to be desired, but for patrons who are willing to scratch the (admittedly dingy) surface and give it a real chance to prove itself, there are tasty rewards to be had . . .

★★★

She wrote a few more sentences, then turned to gaze out the window. The sun was setting over the apartment buildings of Queens, casting them into a dusky golden light. It was almost October now; New York was getting darker earlier each day and growing chillier by the minute. Soon enough, Halloween would be upon them, along with Gladys's deadline for making her decision about the full-time *Standard* job.

She still didn't know what to do. The past two weeks had gone well—she loved reviewing as much as ever, and having Aunt Lydia on her team certainly made getting to restaurants in the city a lot easier. But balancing her *Standard* work with schoolwork and bake sales had been stressful, and she could only imagine how much crazier a full-time workload would be.

Normally, Gladys would turn to an adult for counsel, but since Aunt Lydia had a vested interest in Gladys taking the job, she probably couldn't give selfless advice. Mr. Eng might also see the permanent

Standard job as an excuse to get rid of Aunt Lydia once trade-show season was over, so Gladys wasn't sure she could count on him for impartial guidance, either.

That only left one adult who knew her secret. Gladys thought of the letter she'd received from her former teacher, now hidden in the one place she knew her parents would never snoop: between the pages of a cookbook. Ms. Quincy was wise and well traveled; as a teacher, she clearly believed in a good education, but she also felt strongly about following your passion. Gladys decided she would e-mail her ex-teacher and try to set up a meeting.

The next night, while her parents were out at a movie, Gladys finished her review of Café Havana on the office computer and e-mailed it to Fiona. When that was finished, she started a fresh e-mail.

Dear Ms. Quincy,

Thank you so much for your letter. I would love to meet up and talk. Maybe I can come by East Dumpsford Elementary one day after school this week?

Best,
Gladys

When she logged into DumpMail the following afternoon, she found two new messages in her inbox: one from Ms. Quincy and one from Fiona.

Dear Gladys,

How lovely to hear from you. I have some free time after school tomorrow (Tuesday) if you'd like to stop by. I'm still in Room 116, just like last year.

V. Quincy

Tuesday—that was when Gladys had been hoping to *finally* attend her first meeting of French Club! *I'll just have to put that off for one more week,* she thought. *This is more important.* Gladys fired off a quick response to Ms. Quincy, then clicked over to read her message from Fiona.

Gladys,

Another excellent review from my most dependable critic! Thank you so much for the thoroughness, enthusiasm, and style that you've brought to this series so far.

I really hope that you're still considering the offer I made when we met last month—the *Standard* could use a unique voice like yours on its permanent staff. Let me

know which way you're leaning if you get a chance . . .
and how I can persuade you to change your mind if you're
thinking of turning down the offer.

Cheers,
Fiona

Gladys sighed. It was great to have her talents appreciated, especially since it was a feeling she didn't
always get at home. But it didn't feel so great to know
that Fiona's admiration was still based on a big deception. If Fiona knew how *truly* unique Gladys's voice
was, would she still be so interested in having her at
the paper full-time?

Chapter 20

GREEN PEN, GREEN TEA

WHEN THE LAST BELL RANG THE NEXT afternoon, Gladys was out of the building like a shot. Pedaling the familiar old roads to East Dumpsford Elementary made her feel almost like she was moving backward in time, and when she reached the bike rack in front of the school, it was smaller than she'd remembered. The steps leading up to the front door felt slightly less steep, too. Had the school shrunk? No, she supposed she had grown since the year before.

Gladys's sneakered feet moved silently down the hallway, and she was steps from Room 116 when a sudden feeling of shyness washed over her.

Ms. Quincy was a teacher Gladys admired above any other, and she was glad that she'd offered to advise her. But when she found out how many lies Gladys had told for her job, would she still feel a "rush of pride" for her former student? Maybe coming here hadn't been such a hot idea.

Gladys stopped in her tracks, but when she did, her sneakers let out a loud *squeak!* that echoed around the deserted hallway.

"Gladys?" Ms. Quincy's voice called. "Is that you?"

Fudge. Gladys forced her feet to move into the classroom.

"Gladys! It's wonderful to see you!" The teacher rose from her desk. Her hair was different from how Gladys remembered it—she had gotten rid of her tight curls, opting instead for a super-short buzz cut. But her kooky fashion sense was the same as ever; today she wore pajama-like polka-dotted slacks, strappy brown platform sandals, a bright yellow shirt, and a flowered scarf that fluttered in the breeze from the open window.

"Hi, Ms. Quincy," Gladys said. "Thanks for your letter. It's great to see you, too."

"Have a seat," Ms. Quincy said. "Take any desk you like."

Gladys's feet automatically took her to her old desk, but when she pulled out the chair and sat down, it felt all wrong. The seat was lower to the ground than the seats in middle school. Also, her old desk was stuffed full of a stranger's things, like a sparkly purple pencil case and a folder covered with monster truck stickers.

That combination made it hard to tell whether the desk now belonged to a boy or a girl, but Gladys supposed it didn't really matter—it no longer belonged to her.

Ms. Quincy perched herself on the desk in front of Gladys and brought her sandaled feet up to rest on the short chair. "So, Gladys—or should I call you G?" Ms. Quincy winked. "I read your latest review last week, of Pupuseria El Gran Sabor. It was just wonderful how you described the casamiento as—"

"Ms. Quincy!" Gladys interrupted. If she had to sit there and listen to her teacher heap praise on her writing, she wasn't sure she would be able to admit to her deceptions. "Thanks," she said, "but I don't feel comfortable accepting your compliments. The truth is, I'm a giant fraud."

"A fraud?" Ms. Quincy asked. "What do you mean?"

Gladys plunged in. She told her teacher the whole story of her restaurant-reviewing career: how she had received her first e-mail from Fiona Inglethorpe in the spring; how she had maneuvered her way into the city for her earliest reviews; how she had been afraid to tell her parents about the job and afraid to tell her editor about her age; how her aunt had agreed to help her. "And now," she concluded, "I'm afraid that Fiona will be disappointed if I don't accept the full-time job—and that my aunt will, also, because it's kind of her job now, too." Gladys dug her elbows into her old desk and dropped her forehead into her hands. "I just wanted to be a published food writer, but everything got so complicated." She looked up into Ms. Quincy's kind, dark eyes. "What should I do?"

Ms. Quincy didn't say anything right away. Instead, she rose and walked back over to her desk to retrieve her insulated mug. Gladys wondered if it was still full of gunpowder green tea, which was her teacher's drink of choice. Ms. Quincy took a sip, then brought the mug back with her as she retook her seat in front of Gladys.

"I can't answer that question for you," she said finally. "But I can present you with another one, perhaps a more important one. You seem very concerned about letting other people in your life down. But if you didn't have to worry about what they thought of you, what decisions would you make?"

"I . . ." Gladys was at a loss for how to respond. She had spent so much energy stressing about all the people in her life who seemed impossible to please that she hadn't taken a moment to think about what she actually wanted for herself.

"Spend some time thinking about it," Ms. Quincy said. "In fact . . ." She rose again, looped back to her desk, and returned with a sheet of lined paper and a green gel pen. "I often find that, when faced with difficult decisions, it's best to write out my thoughts and feelings. Sometimes I don't even know how I truly feel until I've written it down. As a writer yourself, I imagine this might help you as well."

Gladys accepted the pen and paper. "I'll give you some time," Ms. Quincy said. "My tea could use a hot-water infusion anyway." She smiled down at Gladys, then stepped out into the hallway with her mug.

Alone in her old classroom, Gladys stared at the blank sheet. She clicked the pen's button and tried to ignore the voice in her head that said, *This is stupid. Writing is what got you into this mess in the first place—it can't help you now.*

"Hush," she said out loud, and touched the pen's point to the paper. She had no idea what she was going to write and thought maybe she'd just doodle for a minute. But the gel ink glided over the paper in such a satisfying way that Gladys soon found herself scribbling line after line.

HONEST THOUGHTS

Middle school—it's tough. Even though I've joined a bunch of clubs, I know I don't fit in. I mean, I didn't fit in in elementary school, either, but middle school is so much bigger that somehow, when I'm not with my friends there, I feel more alone. Plus, there's Elaine de la Vega. Why does she hate me so much? I wish I could figure that out.

The Standard—*I love getting assignments. I love going to restaurants, and really thinking about the food I eat. And I love it when my friends come along to help. I don't want to give up my job, but I'm also not ready for it to become the center of my whole life. I wish I could come up with some sort of compromise that would work for me and for the paper.*

Parents—they still drive me crazy with their bad taste and stupid cooking rules! But if I keep lying to them, I might explode.

Fiona—I'm annoyed that she has such low expectations of kids and what they're willing to eat. I want to find a way to show her that kids can have good taste, too.

Aunt Lydia—I love her, but I can't be responsible for keeping her employed anymore. She needs to find her own path.

And even though I'm still mad at him, I miss Hamilton.

There, she had done it: written out an entire page of completely honest thoughts. She felt a little embarrassed as she read back over some of them (seriously, who in their right mind would turn down a full-time job at the country's most important newspaper to stay in middle school?). But it also felt good to finally be truthful with *someone*. Gladys had been so hung up on her dishonesty to her parents and her editor that she hadn't realized that she wasn't being honest with herself.

She looked up and noticed Ms. Quincy lounging in the classroom doorway. "Well?" the teacher asked. "Did that help at all?"

"It did," Gladys admitted. "The problem is, I don't know how to make it all happen."

"Ah, yes," Ms. Quincy said. "That's the rub. Seeing your goals is the first step. But reaching them often requires taking many more." She approached Gladys's desk again. "The good news is that you don't need to see the entire path clearly to set out on it; you just need to see a few feet ahead of you. Look back over what you wrote. Is there a first step that you can take?"

Gladys stared back down at her list. It looked like she needed to have honest talks with a few people—her parents, her editor, her aunt. But maybe she could warm up by frying a slightly smaller fish: Elaine de la Vega.

"Yeah," Gladys said. "I think I know where to start."

"Just remember, one step at a time," Ms. Quincy said. "If you think about everything that you need to accomplish, it's easy to get overwhelmed. But if you approach your goals bit by bit, you have a good chance of succeeding."

"Thanks, Ms. Quincy," Gladys said. She folded her scribbled-on sheet of paper. "This has been really helpful."

"Anytime," Ms. Quincy said, "and do let me know how it all turns out with your parents and your editor. Because, as your former teacher, I would certainly love to be able to brag openly about your restaurant reviewing if you *do* decide to let your name and age become public information." She smiled, then noticed that Gladys was offering her back her pen. "Oh, you keep that. I can already tell you have an affinity for it."

"Thanks," Gladys said again, and reached for her blue backpack. It didn't have a special pocket for pens and pencils, which was pretty inconvenient; Gladys was often groping through the main compartment at the start of class. For the first time in weeks, she thought of her lobster backpack, and how each of its zippered claws was the perfect size to store writing utensils.

When she got home that afternoon, Gladys dumped the contents of the blue backpack onto her bed and retrieved her lobster from the closet. "You're coming back to school with me tomorrow," Gladys said. "And together, we're going to figure out what to do about Elaine."

Chapter 21

IRRATIONAL DOUGHNUTS

FINDING AN OPPORTUNITY TO CONFRONT Elaine, though, was easier said than done. No sooner had Gladys and her lobster marched into the cafeteria the next day at lunchtime than Shayla from Mathletes waylaid her.

"Gladys!" she cried. "Great news—a slot opened up at the last minute for us to do our bake sale tomorrow. It's either that or wait until December, which will be too late if we want funding to go to that competition on the North Shore."

"Oh . . . right," Gladys said. This was the first she remembered hearing of a competition, but she supposed the Mathletes must have had some good reason for wanting to raise money.

"Great, so we can spend lunch planning!" Shayla grabbed Gladys's elbow and steered her toward an open table. Gladys glanced around the room, but saw no sign of Elaine yet. She sighed, and followed Shayla's lead. Over lunch they discussed different deep-frying oils, and Gladys added notes to her recipe for buñuelo dough after Shayla quintupled each measurement in her head.

That afternoon, Gladys and the Mathletes spent hours mixing, shaping, and frying doughnuts shaped like every digit from one to nine. Plus they rolled some scraps into balls to act as decimals.

Then, the next day at lunchtime, Shayla grabbed Gladys *again,* this time to review the setup for that afternoon's sale.

"So, I thought it would be fun to lay out a whole series of irrational doughnut numbers—like pi, Euler's number, and the square root of two . . ." Shayla started.

Gladys listened for a few moments, but when her eyes started wandering around the cafeteria, her attention quickly followed. Who did Elaine sit with each day? Eighth-graders, surely, but Gladys realized that she had never paid attention to who the *Telegraph* editor hung out with. All the times Elaine had ever accosted her, she had been on her own.

"What do you think?" Shayla asked nervously. "Did we make enough different doughnuts to display each irrational number to twenty decimal places?"

"What? Oh, uh . . ." Gladys looked down at the sheet of notebook paper Shayla had been scribbling on. "Wow," she said. "That's a lot of random numbers! Do they follow any sort of pattern?"

Shayla groaned. "You haven't been listening to me at all. Do you even know what an irrational number is?"

Gladys didn't, and did her best to pay attention to what Shayla was saying for the rest of the lunch period. She still wasn't sure she totally got it in the end, but she at least absorbed enough to understand how Shayla wanted the doughnuts set up at the sale. Gladys warned her that once doughnuts started selling, the number strings would be ruined, but Shayla said she was okay with that as long as they got a picture first.

That afternoon in the lobby, Gladys recruited Charissa to snap some pictures of the doughnut display before the sale officially started. Gladys would have preferred to serve the buñuelos fresh and warm, but there was no way the middle school was going to let them set up a deep fryer full of hot oil in the hallway. The fritters still tasted pretty good, though, considering they had been fried the day before. Gladys had sampled one of the spare doughnut holes to make sure, and she enjoyed the sweet, anise-hinted glaze that had had time to cool and harden on the outside.

As students started to line up to buy doughnuts, Gladys kept a careful eye out for Elaine. The moment she showed up to "cover" this bake sale for the paper, Gladys would pull her aside for a conversation. If there was one thing she knew the Mathletes could handle in her absence, it was totaling up bills and making correct change.

But Elaine never showed, and the next day in the cafeteria, when Gladys was finally free of Shayla, she couldn't spot her, either. Where was she? By the time the period ended, Gladys was resigned to the fact that she wouldn't be able to talk to the girl until next week. In the meantime, she had a Peruvian restaurant to review.

Gladys had had less time this week than the previous ones to do research about the restaurant they'd be visiting, so the next day Sandy suggested that she bring her tablet along on their outing. That way, while Aunt Lydia was sampling wares at her dried-fruit trade show, he and Gladys could peruse the Peruvian restaurant's specialties online.

"Are you sure you won't mind missing the fruits?" Gladys asked him as they made their way from Penn Station to the hotel where the show was being held.

"Nah," Sandy said. "Between the dragon fruit and the durian, fruit hasn't done much for me this year. I'm basically boycotting it now."

"Way to stick it to the fruit," she said.

Still, Sandy was in a good mood. As he'd explained on the train, the dried meats she had brought him had gone a long way to reestablishing his "gross cred" that week at school. Jonah's entry for that round of their competition had been chocolate-covered bacon, a combination he had vastly underestimated. "Everyone actually thought it was good," Sandy explained. "Even Jonah kind of liked it, I could tell. So he's still beating me two rounds to one, but I've got the momentum now. If I can just find one more really awesomely disgusting thing to bring in to school, I might be able to win the title for good!"

"We'll come up with something," Gladys assured him.

Aunt Lydia made sure that they were set up comfortably in some plush chairs in the hotel lobby before she entered the ballroom where the dried-fruit vendors were displaying their wares.

"Okay, here we go!" Sandy spent a few minutes hacking into the hotel's Wi-Fi, and then they navigated straight to the website for Pisco Pisco, their destination for that evening. Luckily, the menu on the website had a lot of pictures.

"Cool. What's that one?" Sandy asked. "It looks like a big plateful of raw fish."

"It's not exactly raw, but it's not cooked," Gladys said, recalling the bit of research she'd been able to squeeze in on Monday. "Ceviche is a popular dish along Peru's coast. The fish is marinated in an acidic solution, which cures it but doesn't cook it."

"Excellent," Sandy murmured. "Okay, that one's definitely a possible candidate for a gross food. Do you think they'd pack it in a doggy bag for me?" He scrolled down. "Whoa—that drink is purple!"

The drink was labeled CHICHA MORADA, so Gladys opened a new tab to do some research about it. It turned out to be a sweet beverage made from purple corn, plus some fruits and spices.

"It's sweet?" Sandy asked. "Then I bet I'll like it. Gross points, zero, but a growing boy does need his sugar." He tapped on the screen to return to the restaurant's menu, but when the next picture filled the screen, he let out a yelp. "What is *that*??"

Gladys looked at the tablet. The picture looked like a roasted rodent on a plate; its head was still on, and you could see its crispy little ears and everything. There was just one word on the screen beneath it: CUY.

Quickly, Gladys did another search, which resulted in several even more horrifying pictures popping up on the screen.

Sandy's eyes were wide with shock, and Gladys suddenly thought of her friend's beloved Edward and Dennis Hopper. Sandy did have some limits when it came to eating meat that might be a close relative of one of his pets. Would cuy be too rabbit-like for him to swallow?

"Look," she said, "this website says that cuy is basically the national dish of Peru . . . but you don't have to eat it. I mean, I probably have to at least try it for my review, but if it freaks you out too much—"

"Freaks me out? Are you kidding?" Sandy turned to her, his wide eyes now sparkling with mischief. "Gatsby, this is the best thing *ever*! Who's even gonna remember the durian when they see me eat a *rat*?"

"Guinea pig," Gladys corrected him. "It looks like cuy is guinea pig."

That information seemed to give Sandy a moment of pause, but soon enough, he shook it off. "Even better," he declared. "So hey, do you think it'll come out looking like this on the plate? All . . . whole and everything?!"

"Um, I guess so," Gladys said. Actually, she didn't think she would mind if it looked a tiny bit *less* like a guinea pig when it arrived on her plate, but she supposed if you were going to be a meat-eater, it was only fair that you should at least occasionally have to look your dinner in its face.

For the rest of the time they spent waiting for Aunt Lydia, the cuy was all Sandy could talk about.

Finally, a subway ride later, they were seated at the restaurant and being served their appetizers. In addition to the ceviche, Gladys had wanted to try a couple of traditional potato dishes: papas rellenas, which were stuffed with meat and deep-fried, and papas a la huancaina, which were cooked in a creamy, cheesy sauce. Taking care to save room in her stomach for all that was to come, Gladys only took a few bites, as did Aunt Lydia, who was already "so stuffed with fruit I feel like a Christmas pie." Sandy, though, was more than happy to vacuum up the rest, "to clear space for the main event."

More dishes came out, and Gladys began to take notes on how Peruvian cuisine was different from Salvadoran and Cuban—which was the whole point of her multi-restaurant series. Finally, the dish they had been waiting for arrived at their table, the whole cuy on it split and splayed out like a much tinier version of a roasted pig.

Aunt Lydia sat up straighter. "Now *that* looks interesting!"

Gladys reached into her lobster for her tablet. "You want me to take a video?" she asked Sandy. "You know, that you can show your classmates?"

To her surprise, he shook his head. In fact, he was looking a little hesitant now. "Uh . . ." he said. "Why don't you go first, Gatsby? I mean, you should get to taste it while it's . . . you know . . . hot and everything."

His voice cracked on the last word. Gladys turned to Aunt Lydia, who nodded encouragingly. It looked like it was all on her to get this cuy-eating party started.

"Okay," she said, "anyone who doesn't want to see this, avert your eyes." Then, with a deep breath, Gladys grabbed her sharp knife and sawed off one of the cuy's legs. *It's just like eating a chicken drumstick,* she told

herself as she raised the small joint to her lips. *Like a tiny little chicken drumstick.* She took a bite.

She chewed—then chewed some more. The meat was tougher than she'd expected. *You just have to get one bite down,* she told herself. *Just this one bite.* Finally, with a small shudder, she swallowed.

"Whoa," Sandy said softly. "So *that's* how a professional does it. Gatsby, I'm inspired!" Reaching forward, he cut off another leg for himself, and Aunt Lydia followed.

"Excuse me," Gladys said. "I . . . um . . . have to go make some notes." Then she ran off to the bathroom with her journal before she had to watch the others bite into their meat.

When she got back to the table, Sandy was tossing a bare bone down onto his plate and accepting a takeout box from the waiter. "I assume you're done with this, right?" he asked Gladys, pointing to the rest of the cuy. She nodded, and then, in one fell swoop, Sandy lifted the guinea pig up off its platter and dumped it into the Styrofoam clamshell. "Then you don't mind if I take it in with me for lunch on Monday, do you? Jonah's gonna *freak out* when he sees me take a bite out of this thing . . . especially if I start with the face!"

Gladys could only imagine what Parm would say in this situation. She was happy when Sandy snapped the lid into place so that she didn't have to look at the cuy anymore. Soon enough, her appetite returned and she was able to sample some of the lomo saltado, whose plain old beef thankfully had no skin, bones, or claws, and was stir-fried to tender perfection.

The next day, as part of her review for the *New York Standard* Dining section, G. Gatsby e-mailed her editor the following words:

> *Cuy is a favorite traditional food of many Peruvians. With its thick-skinned, rubbery texture and gamey flavor, it seems unlikely to win a lot of American fans, though it is certainly a novelty. If you order it, you may find yourself in a game of chicken with your dining companions over who is brave enough to taste it first . . . and those who do partake may find themselves wishing that they had actually ordered the chicken instead.*
>
>

Chapter 22

ONE FISH FRIED

WHEN ELAINE ONCE AGAIN FAILED TO make an appearance at lunch on Monday, Gladys had to reconsider her plan to confront the girl. After all, Elaine hadn't showed up at her last bake sale, and hadn't bothered her in over a week. Maybe she'd decided to give up whatever vendetta she had against Gladys.

But then, when she remembered the article Elaine had written about her in the *Telegraph*—and the threat she'd made about keeping an eye on Gladys going forward—her resolve steeled again. Elaine was probably trying to trick Gladys into *thinking* she'd given up, while really she was lying low like a snake in the grass, waiting for her next opportunity to strike. And Gladys refused to remain on the defensive.

But that didn't mean she wasn't nervous as she approached the Media Room door after school. Pulling Elaine aside at lunchtime or at a bake sale was one thing, but now Gladys was about to walk into a meeting of the club Elaine was in charge of. She'd be on Elaine's turf, surrounded by Elaine's friends. The thought was almost enough to make Gladys turn tail and run in the other direction.

Instead, she took a deep breath and stroked her lobster's fuzzy strap for comfort. Then, drawing up every last ounce of resolve she had, she opened the Media Room door.

The room was crowded with equipment—computers, scanners, and printers took up just about every inch of table space—but the one thing it was not crowded with was people. In fact, there was only one other person in the room: Elaine de la Vega, typing away at a computer with her back to the entrance.

Gladys cleared her throat, and Elaine swiveled around in her chair.

"Uh, hi," Gladys said. "I thought there was a newspaper meeting here today. Is it canceled?"

"You're here to join the newspaper?" Elaine asked. Her expression was incredulous.

Gladys shook her head. "Actually, I just came here to talk to you. I thought I might be interrupting your meeting, but I guess you moved it?"

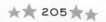

Elaine glanced around the room, quiet except for the low hum of machines. "Clearly, you're not interrupting anything."

Gladys had really lucked out—she wouldn't have to make a scene after all. "Can I sit down?" she asked.

Elaine shrugged. "It's a free country."

Gladys pulled a swivel chair out from one of the other computer stations and dropped her backpack to the floor. She sat down, and her voice shook slightly as she said the words she'd been practicing in her head all week. "I wanted to talk to you because it's pretty clear that you hate me. What's not clear to me, though, is why." It was a hard thing for her to say, but an honest one. The question was, would Elaine be honest in return?

Elaine stared at Gladys for a long moment. "I don't hate you," she said finally. "But what I do hate is watching someone with talent waste their potential on activities they *clearly* have no interest in."

Gladys frowned. "Is this about the bake sales?"

Elaine gave her a withering look. "Of course it's about the bake sales. I *discovered* you on the first day of school, writing that opinion piece about school lunches. I *told* you you'd make an excellent addition to the newspaper staff, but you said you were too busy to write for the *Telegraph*. Then you turned around and joined every other club under the sun, and even wasted your time helping clubs you weren't in! I don't get it, Gladys." Now Elaine's voice wavered. "Did someone warn you to stay away from me or something?"

Gladys had never thought about things this way—had never considered that *Elaine's* feelings might have been hurt by her decision to join all those other clubs. "But why would you care that much if one person chooses not to join the paper?" Gladys said. "You must have a huge staff of writers to manage already."

Elaine snorted. "Look around you, Gladys. I have *no* staff. The meeting didn't get moved to another day—this *is* the meeting. It's just that nobody ever shows up."

Gladys could hardly believe what she was hearing. "What?"

"The *DTMS Telegraph* is just me," Elaine said. "I mean, a few seventh-graders showed up for the first meeting of the year, but none of them came back. And all the eighth-graders who were on the paper staff last year quit. It's not me who hates you. It's everyone at this school who hates me."

"That can't be true," Gladys said—but, now that she thought about it, she realized she had never actually seen Elaine hanging out with anyone else at DTMS.

"It is true, and I'm used to it," Elaine spat. "When I saw you sitting alone, writing in that journal, I thought you might be different—might be a worthy partner. But you turned out to be just like everybody else."

Gladys picked her lobster backpack up off the floor.

"Do you remember this?" she asked. "You made a comment about it at orientation. It upset me. *That* was why I didn't want to join your paper—well, that, and because you read my private writing over my shoulder instead of asking first. Maybe if you didn't do stuff like that, people wouldn't have such a bad first impression of you."

"I have strong opinions," Elaine retorted. "I'm forceful and decisive. That's what makes me a good leader."

"Yeah, but it's hard to be a leader if you can't inspire anyone to follow you."

Elaine glanced around the empty Media Room. "I guess that's true." She sighed. "My big hope was to produce a really incredible first issue—and then, when everyone saw how great the paper was, they'd want to join. What I *really* wanted was to have high-quality color photos, but the paper doesn't have the budget for color printing." She looked up at Gladys. "I don't know why I'm even telling you this."

"If you need more money for color printing, why don't you hold a fund-raiser?" Gladys asked.

"I'm no baker," Elaine said. "And even if I was, where would I find the time? Producing an entire newspaper is a lot of work for one person. I even got special permission from Dr. Sloane to spend my lunch periods in here working, but I'm still behind schedule."

So that was why Elaine had been absent from the cafeteria last week. "Look," Gladys said. "My own schedule should be clearing up next week. If you need some help—"

But Elaine cut her off. "Thanks, Gladys, but I'm not gonna sell your pity cookies. No offense."

Gladys bristled at this, but then decided to let it go. Elaine clearly still had some work to do on her people skills—but she had been honest with Gladys, and that was all Gladys had wanted. Their conversation had gone about as well as she could have hoped.

"Okay," she said, "but I'm not sure that a bake sale would be the best fund-raising fit for the paper, anyway. It would make more sense to come up with something that would provide a steady stream of income for the *Telegraph* going forward."

The scowl disappeared from Elaine's face, and she leaned forward in her seat. "All right, I'm listening."

Gladys leaned in, too. "Why don't you sell advertising space instead? You could get ads from local businesses . . . and you could even ask clubs to pay to advertise their meeting days, too. That bulletin board outside the cafeteria is getting pretty crowded—it's hard to keep track of which group meets when."

Elaine cocked her head to one side, considering. "That's actually not a terrible idea."

Gladys figured that was the closest to a compliment she was going to get from this girl. "I'm glad I could help." She rose to her feet. "All right, I'd better let you get back to work. Oh, and if you need some photos of the Mathletes bake sale for an article or something, Charissa Bentley has some on her phone."

"Good to know," Elaine said. Gladys was two steps from the door when Elaine spoke again. "And Gladys . . ."

Gladys turned back to her.

Elaine's cheeks colored, but she continued to speak anyway. "I really am sorry about that article about you. I let my resentment eclipse my commitment to responsible journalism, and that's not okay."

"Thanks for saying that," Gladys said quietly.

They both stood there awkwardly for a moment, then Gladys stepped forward and offered her hand. Elaine took it, and they shook.

"Good luck with the new edition," Gladys said. "I look forward to reading it."

When she reached her locker, Gladys unzipped one of her lobster's claw pockets and pulled out Ms. Quincy's green pen. She then pulled out her page of honest thoughts and reread the first paragraph.

Plus, there's Elaine de la Vega. Why does she hate me so much? I wish I could figure that out.

Gladys drew a thin line through those words.

One fish fried. Four more to go.

Chapter 23

THE MACARONS OF PEACE

SANDY WAS WAITING ON GLADYS'S front stoop when she got home. "I did it!" he cried. "Operation Eat the Rodent's Face Off was a success!"

"Really?!" Disgusted as she was by the name he had given his mission, Gladys was thrilled to hear Sandy's good news. "Tell me everything!"

Sandy beamed as Gladys took a seat next to him. "Jonah had no chance! Though what he brought in was actually kind of cool. It was this little pill made from a berry from West Africa, and taking it makes sour foods taste really sweet for about half an hour. So after he took it, he ate a lemon—the flesh and everything—and then drank a whole cupful of vinegar."

"A cup of vinegar?" Gladys's stomach

gave a lurch. "That *is* pretty gross." The berry sounded fascinating, though—she'd definitely have to do more research on it.

"It was nasty," Sandy agreed, "so he did get some points. Just not as many as me. I mean, I ate the cuy in front of everyone without taking any sort of cheaty pill first! Xavier Martin was so disgusted, he had to run to the nurse's office to puke." Sandy beamed at this accomplishment.

"Well, if that's the test, then it sounds like you passed with flying colors," Gladys said.

"I'll be known as Rat-Boy forever," Sandy said proudly. "Already a legend at St. Joe's! Though I couldn't have done it without you, Gatsby. Thanks again for all the help. You can totally claim the title of Rat-Girl if you want."

Gladys had to smile at that. "So, how did you celebrate? Did the other boys hoist you up onto their shoulders and parade you around? Did someone make you a crown?"

"Yeah, and they sang 'Rat-Boy Is Our King,' too." Sandy laughed. "Is that really what you think people do at private school? You read too much Harry Potter."

She shoved him. "Don't mock the Potter."

"Okay, okay—joking!" Sandy held up his hands in surrender. "So hey, your last review is in. What are you going to tell Fiona about the full-time job?"

"I have some ideas," Gladys said, though that was

a bit of an exaggeration. She had precisely one idea—but she thought it had some potential.

"Cryptic," Sandy said. "So you're not gonna tell me?"

Gladys sighed. "I just think this is a step I'm going to have to take on my own."

He nodded. "Fair enough. Just don't go doing anything stupid, like spilling the beans to your parents first."

Gladys didn't say anything. Sandy was probably right; it probably was a stupid idea. But that was exactly what she was planning to do.

Gladys knew the whole parental situation had to be handled with care, and she decided to talk to them on a night when she could cook some of their favorite foods. She also thought it would be best to do it without Aunt Lydia present. Since her aunt had one last foodie trade show to attend that coming Saturday afternoon, Gladys planned to wait until the weekend to have the discussion.

But then, that Friday after school, something unexpected happened.

Gladys was once again behind the bake sale table, this time with the Chess Club. Jason Mitty had purchased silicone molds online, and Gladys and the other members had spent the previous evening at his house, microwaving dark and white chocolate chunks and filling the molds to create edible chess pieces. It had been one of her easier projects to oversee, especially since there was no baking, icing, or frying involved.

She was just wrapping up the white-chocolate knight Parm had bought for Charissa ("You know, to say thanks for last time," Parm said) when she noticed a figure lurking just outside the lobby's smudged glass doors. She couldn't see his face, but he was dressed all in black.

It's not him, Gladys told herself. *You're hallucinating.* Besides, even though this person was wearing a hat, it wasn't Hamilton's signature fedora; it was a black beret, like the kind poets and painters wore. Maybe it was someone from the Art Club, Gladys thought, come to spy on her and find out why she was skipping today's meeting.

She kept selling chess pieces, waiting for the figure to come into the building or leave. But it didn't do either. Finally, Gladys's curiosity got the better of her.

"Hey, Jason, can you handle things for a while?" she asked. The boy said he could, and Gladys headed for the exit. She pushed open the door and stepped out into the October chill.

"Gladys."

She knew that voice; what she didn't know was how to react to it. The same old mix of contradictory emotions flooded through her: happiness and annoyance. Relief and fury. If there was one thing she knew, though, it was that this time, she wasn't going to run away from her feelings. She turned to Hamilton and looked him straight in the face.

"Hey," she said. "New hat?"

Hamilton reached up and touched the rim of the beret. "I got it in Paris," he said. "It was a gift from my French publisher, actually. They flew me out the same night I came here for the school assembly, and I only just got back." He glanced down at the black-banded watch on his wrist. "Like, an hour ago."

Gladys nodded slowly. Hamilton had been out of the country; that explained a few things. Though they had phones and Internet in France, didn't they?

She reminded herself not to jump to any conclusions. Unlike last time, she should at least give Hamilton a chance to explain himself. She glanced back inside, but it looked like Jason and the rest of the Chess Club had the sale under control. "Want to take a walk?" Gladys asked. "I could show you around."

As soon as she said that, though, she felt stupid. Why would a boy who had just gotten off a plane from Paris want a tour of the local middle school? "Never mind," she said quickly. "There's nothing to see, unless you want to watch the sports teams practicing or something."

"No, that sounds great!" Hamilton protested. "I've never seen a middle-school sports team practice. It'll be a new experience for me."

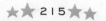

Gladys blinked in surprise. "Okay, then." She led the way down the steps and around the side of the building.

She must have been striding quickly, because Hamilton had to jog a few steps to catch up with her. "Hey, so, I brought you something from France," he said. Gladys slowed as he reached into his black messenger bag and pulled out a long rectangular box. It was made of clear plastic, and held an assortment of perfectly circular, rainbow-colored cookies.

"They're called macarons," he said.

"I know what macarons are," she replied, though she left out the fact that the recipe had given her fits on the first day of school.

"They sell them all over," Hamilton said. "Even in gift shops at the airport. But I got these from a town called Montmorillon, about three hours outside of Paris. They're supposed to make the best in the country."

They had just come to the edge of an empty field. The teams that were practicing were a bit farther out, but Gladys stopped walking.

"Hamilton," she said, "you didn't have to bring me a fancy present. I mean, don't get me wrong—these macarons look incredible. But I would have been happy if you had just called me once after camp ended . . . or answered one of my e-mails."

"One of your e-mails?" Hamilton looked confused. "But I didn't get any e-mails from you."

Yeah, sure, Gladys thought.

"What address did you use?"

"The one I found on ZombietownUSA.com."

Hamilton groaned softly. "Gladys, that e-mail address is for *fans.* Do you have any idea how many messages go to that account every day?"

Gladys didn't have any idea—and found that, actually, she didn't really want to know.

"And anyway," Hamilton continued, "those e-mails don't come to me; they go to my publicist. She hardly ever forwards any to me. Most go into a long queue and get answered with some kind of generic response."

Gladys let out a puff of air, blowing her bangs out of her eyes. "But I clearly said in the e-mails that I was your friend," she told him, "and that I needed to get in touch with you urgently!"

"That's what they *all* say." Hamilton sighed. "How was my publicist supposed to know that of all the people who write and claim to be a close friend with an urgent message, you were the one telling the truth?"

Now that Hamilton had explained it, Gladys supposed it did make some sense that her e-mails wouldn't have gotten through the gatekeeper. So he hadn't known she was trying to contact him.

"Okay, well, I called your house, too," she told him.

"My parents came with me to France," Hamilton replied, "so no one would have been home to answer."

"And what about before then?" she asked. "I gave

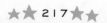

you my number on the last day of camp. How come you never called *me*?"

Now a blush crept up over the rim of Hamilton's black turtleneck, and he leaned against the outer wall of the school. "I'm so embarrassed," he said, "but your number . . . it got destroyed."

"Destroyed?"

"Well, you *did* write it on a napkin," he retorted. "Not exactly the sturdiest surface in the world."

A twinge of annoyance shot through Gladys— probably because Hamilton was right. She had grabbed at the first thing she saw in the camp kitchen when he'd asked for her number. Still, she felt weirdly defensive about it. "I'm sorry," she said, a snide note sneaking into her voice, "but not all of us are lucky enough to have a three-hundred-page novel to record our numbers in for posterity. *Some* of us just use whatever materials we have around."

To her surprise, Hamilton nodded; he seemed content to concede the point. "I should have been more careful with it," he said, and he really did look pained about the whole thing. "But I stuck it in my jeans pocket, and, well, if you remember, that day was a real scorcher. By the time I got home, the ink had bled and the napkin was in tatters."

Gladys shook her head. Heaven forbid Hamilton should ever consider wearing weather-appropriate clothes—like shorts—when it got hot out.

"I tried to find your number online and in the phone book," he continued, "but your family's unlisted. So then I just kept hoping you would call me, but you never did."

"I figured you were busy writing," Gladys said. "I didn't want to be a nuisance."

Hamilton glanced down at his black boots. "You couldn't be a nuisance."

Now it was Gladys's turn to blush—and her face grew even hotter when she remembered how she had stomped away from Hamilton at school weeks ago. "So when you came here to do the school assembly . . ." she started.

"Well, I couldn't get in touch with you," he said, "but I knew that you went to public school in East Dumpsford. So I asked my publicist to book a school visit for me here. I figured it was my best chance of . . . you know . . ."

Gladys stared at him. "Are you saying that you set up that whole assembly *just* in the hopes of bumping into me?"

Hamilton stood up a bit straighter. "Of course," he replied. "Do you think I *like* showing a slide show about my life to kids my own age? I know no one here wants to see that. Ugh, it's humiliating!"

"Huh." Maybe Hamilton wasn't quite as socially clueless as Gladys had initially imagined.

"I tried one more time to track you down from

France," Hamilton said, "just by doing a search online for your name. But I couldn't find any information. In fact, the only person who kept popping up was this writer for the *New York Standard* named G. Gatsby. Who, by the way, is a big fan of Cape Flats, that South African restaurant we went to together. Have you seen the review?"

"Hamilton," Gladys said, exasperated. "I *wrote* that review! *I'm* G. Gatsby!"

Fudge—she certainly hadn't meant to let it just slip out like that.

"What?" Hamilton said. "You're a reporter for the *New York Standard*?"

"Restaurant critic," Gladys corrected him. "Just freelance for now, though that could change. Not a lot of people know, though, so if you could, um, not tell anyone . . ."

"Of course," Hamilton said. "Wow. You know, I read all of G. Gatsby's—I mean, your—reviews. They were really good. I almost tried to contact them through the paper to see if they were a relative of yours or something."

Gladys sighed. "Sounds like we just kept missing each other."

"Well, it's all worked out in the end," Hamilton said, chancing a tentative smile. "When I got home from the airport, I finally heard your message. I figured there might still be time to catch you at school. And here we are now, two old friends, together again."

"Two old friends," Gladys repeated. She realized that Hamilton was still holding out the box of macarons. She accepted it, taking care not to jostle the delicate cookies or touch Hamilton's long fingers. *Friends,* she repeated to herself.

She took a deep breath. "Hamilton, I'm sorry for the way I treated you that day you came to school. I should have stopped and listened instead of jumping to conclusions. I . . . I guess I was just upset, because I assumed you had forgotten all about me."

Hamilton shook his head. "I couldn't forget about you, Gladys."

And just like that, the space between them was closed, and he had swept her up in an enormous hug. Gladys embraced him back, standing on her tiptoes. Over his shoulder, she spotted the girls' soccer team pouring out of the gym doors and onto the field for their drills; any moment, they'd be surrounded.

"Come on," she said. "Let me walk you home. Where *do* you live, by the way?"

"It's not far," Hamilton said. "I'll show you." And they set off together toward the gap in the chain-link fence that surrounded the field.

Chapter 24

LIKE A SHAKEN-UP SODA

THE SIDE STREET THEY HAD EXITED ONTO was quiet; most of the other kids caught a bus home or got picked up in front of the school.

"So," Gladys said, "are you back in East Dumpsford for good?"

"For now," Hamilton replied. "When the sequel is published, I'll have to head back onto the road—my fans demand it." He didn't sound so excited about it, though. "You know, I think you have the right idea, Gladys, publishing somewhat anonymously. You get all the pleasure of practicing your craft without having it completely upend your normal life."

"You think my life is normal?" Gladys laughed. "My parents have no idea I've been writing for the *Standard*. Try sneaking into the city every time you have a restaurant to visit, and sneaking onto the computer at home every time you need to type something up. Plus, my editor thinks I'm a professional adult writer; she has no idea I'm just a kid."

"All right," Hamilton said. "I suppose that sounds a bit more complicated than I imagined. But at least you're able to go to a regular school. Other than at my assembly and in a few movies, I've never even seen one." He sighed. "I passed a bulletin board on my way into the auditorium that day, and it was filled with notices for the most fascinating-sounding activities. Debate Club. French Club. You know, I picked up a little while I was on tour in France—it would be nice to learn more."

"You can't study French as part of your home-schooling?" Gladys asked as they turned a corner.

"Oh, I could," Hamilton said, "but it would still be nice to have other people my age to practice with."

Gladys nodded. It would be nice if, one of these days, *she* could find the time to go to a French Club meeting, too.

"But it's not just that. I also saw a flyer for the Halloween dance your school is having in a couple of weeks. I've never been to a dance," Hamilton said sadly.

"Hamilton," Gladys said, "you've been on TV. You've been to *Europe*. You really want to go to a middle-school dance?"

Hamilton stopped short and turned to face her. "Are you asking me to the dance, Gladys Gatsby?"

Gladys blushed all over again. That hadn't been her intention—but Hamilton clearly wanted to go. Was that what she wanted, too?

"Um, sure," she said. "Do you wanna go with me?"

Hamilton grinned. "I'd love to. I'll wear my finest suit."

"Actually, I think you're supposed to wear a costume," Gladys said. "Since it's Halloween and all."

"Right. Well, I'll come up with something."

They resumed their stroll through the neighborhood, walking another half block in silence. Gladys had one more thing that she wanted to ask Hamilton, but she had to work up her courage. Finally, she spoke.

"Hamilton," she said, "are things any better with your parents now? You know, since you told them how you felt about them not supporting your career?"

Hamilton frowned, thinking for a moment. "I think so," he said finally. "After all, they did both come to France with me, which I don't think they would have done if I hadn't said I wanted them to. So I'm glad I told them how I felt."

Gladys nodded. She was glad to hear that Hamilton's discussion with his parents had been successful. It gave her some hope for her own.

"There's my house," he said, pointing out a squat

white ranch with gingerbread trim. It was more modest than Gladys had expected; for some reason she'd imagined Hamilton living in a mansion in The Seabreeze, Charissa's posh neighborhood. Hamilton seemed to sense Gladys's surprise. "I know, not necessarily the abode you'd expect for an internationally best-selling author. But my parents insist that I save all my book earnings for college."

"That sounds smart," Gladys said.

Hamilton shrugged. "I keep trying to tell them that one dirt bike won't stop me from being able to pay for Harvard, but so far, they've been strict."

"A dirt bike?" That didn't fit with Gladys's image of Hamilton at all. "You know you can't wear a fedora or a beret under your helmet, right?"

A smile crossed Hamilton's face. "Yes, I know."

"Well, if you get them to change their minds, I'll have to introduce you to my friend Sandy. He'll definitely want a ride."

They were standing at the base of Hamilton's driveway now; he pulled a cell phone out of his pocket. "Just got this in September," he explained. "You'd better give me your phone number one more time—and your e-mail—so we don't fall out of touch all over again."

Gladys gave him her contact information gladly, then pulled out her reviewing notebook and green pen to take his.

"No cell for you?" he asked.

She shook her head. "My parents say not 'til I'm thirteen. I don't mind, though." Or she hadn't, at least, until this moment. Suddenly, she thought she might like to have a way to exchange a few private texts.

"Well," Hamilton said, "I guess I'll see you at the dance, if not sooner. Shall I pick you up beforehand?"

"Nah, it's out of your way," Gladys said. "We can just meet at the school."

"Until then," Hamilton said.

Gladys set off down the street. Thinking about potentially dancing with Hamilton on Halloween kind of made her feel like a shaken-up can of soda—so instead, all the way home, she tried to focus on what he had said about talking with his parents. It had worked for him. Would it work for her, too?

By the time she got to her house, a new idea was knocking around in her head. She hurried straight to the office and picked up the phone to dial the number she had written in her journal only a short while earlier.

"Hamilton?" she said when she got him on the phone. "I have an idea, and I was hoping you might help me." She took a deep breath. "What are you doing tomorrow night?"

Chapter 25

SPILLING THE BEANS

GLADYS WAS SETTING THE TABLE THAT Saturday evening when her mom wandered into the dining room. "Four places?" she asked. "But your aunt's working in the city tonight. It'll just be the three of us."

"Actually," Gladys said, "I invited a friend over. I hope that's okay."

"A friend?" Her mom suddenly perked up. "Well, sure, honey, that sounds great." As if on cue, the doorbell rang.

"I'll get it!" Gladys's dad called. A moment later, he appeared in the dining room entryway, his voice lowered to a whisper. "Jen!" he hissed. "It's that author kid—the one who wrote *Zombietown, U.S.A.*!"

"Hamilton Herbertson?" Gladys's mom gasped.

"He told me Gladdy invited him for dinner."

"I did," Gladys said. "We became friends at camp, remember?"

Gladys's dad looked down at his Saturday sweat-pants and shook his head. "I wish you'd told me sooner, Gladdy. I would have gotten dressed."

"Oh, Hamilton doesn't care about those things," Gladys said, though as the words came out, she wondered if they were true. Hamilton did have a very strict dress code for himself.

"Well, what are you waiting for?" Gladys's mom said to her dad. "Offer the boy a soda or something!"

"Or you could just invite him in here," Gladys said. "Dinner's ready."

As Gladys's dad led him into the dining room, Hamilton caught her eye and smiled. He was dressed in his usual black, and carried a bright bouquet of flowers that he presented to Gladys's mom. *Smooth,* Gladys thought. They hadn't planned that detail, but it was a clever move on Hamilton's part. "How very polite!" Gladys's mom exclaimed, her eyes shining as she left to put the flowers in some water.

A few minutes later, everyone was seated, and the meal Gladys made was laid out on the table. The dinner was an eclectic one: she'd baked a pizza with three cheeses and bacon (her dad's favorite from the now-defunct Pathetti's); she'd roasted asparagus (her mom's favorite vegetable) with olive oil and salt; and she'd oven-baked French fries (everyone's favorite!) with a side of spicy aioli. Her parents happily gobbled up everything she put on their plates, and Hamilton answered as many questions as they could throw at him about his career as a child author and what might be coming next for the characters of their favorite novel.

Finally, when everyone's stomach was full, it was time for Gladys and Hamilton to put their plan into action.

"You know, Mr. and Mrs. Gatsby," Hamilton said, "I'm not the only young writer in this room."

"Oh, yes, we know that," Gladys's dad said. "Our Gladdy is very talented. Her sixth-grade teacher read us something she wrote for a contest last year, and it was really very good."

Gladys's mom agreed with a smile.

"Well," Hamilton continued, "I think that people who are good writers deserve to have their work published for others to read. Don't you think so?"

"Oh, absolutely," Gladys's mom said.

Gladys crossed her toes inside her sneakers. Hamilton had done a great job of setting her up, but now it was her turn to talk.

"Mom, Dad," she said, "what would you say if I told you I had a chance to write about food for a real newspaper?"

"For the school paper?" Gladys's mom asked. Gladys shook her head.

"What, then—for the *Intelligencer*?" Gladys's dad asked, referring to the local paper. "Are they starting up a student opinions column or something?"

"That sounds like a great idea," her mom said.

"It's not for the *Intelligencer*," Gladys said. The moment of truth had finally arrived. "It's for the *New York Standard*."

"The *Standard*?" Gladys's dad took off his glasses. "How on earth would that have come about?"

"It's a long story," Gladys said.

"I don't doubt it." Gladys's father rubbed his eyes, then put his glasses back on. "You know how we feel about that newspaper here in East Dumpsford, Gladdy. They weren't very nice the last time they wrote about our town."

"I know," Gladys said. "But do you think you might be willing to give them another chance? Especially if they were the publisher of your own daughter's restaurant reviews?"

"Restaurant reviews? Gladys, what are you talking about?" Her mom glanced confusedly at Hamilton. "Do you have some sort of connection there, Hamilton?"

"No, Mom," Gladys said. "He had nothing to do with it. Hang on."

She left the table and crossed into the living room, her legs quaking beneath her with each step. Her parents were going to have to see the evidence. She reached under the couch for the papers she had stashed there two months earlier, still open to the Dining section.

When she handed them to her parents, they still had baffled expressions on their faces.

"Just look," Gladys said, and miraculously, without asking any more questions, they did.

She had just enough time to exchange a worried glance with Hamilton before her dad lowered his paper to the table.

"These are all those hot dog places we visited together over the summer," he said. "G. Gatsby—is that you?"

"Well, it's certainly not *you*, George," Gladys's mom said, lowering her own paper. She stared at her daughter, then turned to Hamilton. "Hamilton," she said, "would you mind excusing us for a moment?"

"Of course not." Hamilton quickly pushed his chair back, and Gladys's heart sank. She had hoped that having him around would keep things from getting too ugly. But she supposed it was fair for her parents to want to talk to her alone.

Gladys's mom waited until he'd left the room before she spoke again. "You had an article published in the *New York Standard*?" she asked quietly. She looked back at the top of the newspaper page in her hand. "In *August*? Gladys, why didn't you tell us?"

"I was going to," Gladys said. "I was all set to tell you the day the review came out. But that was the day

Aunt Lydia got here, and things got complicated." She looked down at her plate. "But that's not the whole truth. I've had other reviews published before that one, and after, too."

"How many?" her dad asked.

"Six," Gladys admitted. "The first one was of Classy Cakes, the restaurant I visited with Charissa on her birthday, back in April."

"April!" Gladys's mom cried. "So this has been going on for more than six months?"

"It's been a while," Gladys admitted. "I'm sorry. I didn't mean to keep it a secret for so long. I was just worried about how you would react. You were so angry last year when you found out I'd been cooking behind your backs . . ."

"We were angry because you set the kitchen on fire," Gladys's mom corrected her. "And because you seemed . . . well . . . overly obsessed with cooking. We wanted to make sure you weren't missing out on your childhood. This, though"—she glanced back down at the newspaper—"well, this situation seems a bit different." She leaned forward. "Can you tell us more about it? How did you get this job? What other restaurants have you reviewed?"

And so Gladys spilled the beans. She explained about the mix-up that happened when she entered the *New York Standard* student essay contest. And about accepting the Classy Cakes assignment, and getting to eat there thanks to Charissa's birthday reservation. And how that had inspired her to request her own birthday outing to Fusión Tapas (review #2), how she had written all about the hot dogs they'd eaten together that summer (review #3), and how she'd been visiting Latin American restaurants with Aunt Lydia and publishing write-ups of them after (reviews #4, #5, and #6).

"So Lydia knew about all of this?" Gladys's mom asked.

Gladys winced—she knew this would be a sore point with her parents. It was part of the reason she hadn't wanted Aunt Lydia to be home when she told them.

"Yes," she said, "and so did Mr. Eng. They're both foodies, so I felt like I could trust them . . ."

"But you couldn't trust us," Gladys's dad said.

"I'm trusting you now," Gladys said in a shaky voice. "I know I should have told you sooner, but I hope that my coming clean with you now counts for something." She took a deep breath to get her voice back under control. "I've always been responsible about my reviews. I've always had someone else with me. I've never snuck off into the city by myself. And I didn't lie to my editor at first about my age; I just . . . didn't correct her when she assumed I was older than I am. But I don't want to keep secrets anymore." She looked up at both of her parents with pleading eyes. "I really liked it when we spent time together this summer looking for fun hot dogs. Wouldn't it be nice if we could keep doing that kind of thing? As a family?"

Her question hung in the air like ripe fruit on a drooping branch.

Gladys's parents were doing the thing where they communicated silently with each other through raised eyebrows and lip twitches. Finally, her father spoke.

"I'm afraid this kind of deception just can't be tolerated, Gladdy." His expression was grim. "It seems that our last punishment didn't do the trick. This time, we'll have to restrict you to your room."

"What?" Gladys's voice sounded so small, she hardly recognized it.

"Yes," her mom said. "And once again, there will be *nothing* for you to eat but Sticky Burger, Palace of Wong, Fred's Fried Fowl, and our own miserable cooking."

Wait—had her mom just cracked a smile?

"And," her dad continued, "whenever your mom and I cook, we'll torture you by making you listen to all our mistakes without ever being allowed to come down and help, and— Jen, you're ruining it!"

Gladys's mom was laughing now. "I'm sorry!" she gasped. "I tried to keep a straight face, I really did!" Now Gladys's dad was chuckling, too.

"What's going on?" Gladys asked. Suddenly, she was the only stone-faced one in the room.

"Oh, Gladdy," her dad said, "we're just messing with

you. Look at this!" He shook his copy of the paper. "Multiple articles in the *New York Standard,* and all written while you were also going to school or camp! How could we punish you for that?"

"We're proud," her mom said. "So proud." Her eyes were teary now—probably from all the laughter, but maybe not.

"Really?" Gladys could hardly let herself believe what she was hearing.

"Really." Her mom launched out of her seat to smother Gladys in a hug. Her dad swooped in as well, and Gladys felt like a mini hot dog, all wrapped up in a puff pastry of love. Suddenly her eyes were full of tears, too.

She had told the truth, and everything was okay.

Well, almost everything.

"I still need to talk to my editor," Gladys said when her parents released her. "I want to come clean with her, too." She turned to her dad. "Do you think you could take me back to the *New York Standard* building on a weekday?"

"Don't you have school?" her dad asked.

"Well, yeah," Gladys said, "but if we went on Halloween, I wouldn't miss much. Half my classes are just having parties that day, anyway. So as long as I could get home in time for the dance that night . . ." She blushed then, thinking about Hamilton sitting quietly in the next room.

"I think it's okay, George," Gladys's mom said. "One day off from school won't kill her."

"All right," her dad said. "You set it up, and I'll get you to the *Standard* building."

The plan was fixed. Gladys called Hamilton back into the dining room, then retrieved dessert: the box of macarons he had given her the day before. Gladys's mom went straight for the pink one, which turned out to be cherry, while her dad selected a pale green pistachio cookie. There were no black cookies for Hamilton, so he picked a deep purple one, while Gladys plucked out one that was orange in both hue and flavor.

She grinned at Hamilton, and he shot her back a purple-tinged smile. Like making macarons, tonight's operation had required delicacy and precision—but together, they had pulled it off with flying colors.

Gladys met Aunt Lydia on the porch when she got home that night. She had saved her aunt several macarons—the boldest colors—and waited to hear all about that day's sheep-and-goat-cheese convention before filling her in on what happened over dinner.

"I'm sorry I didn't tell you what I was planning," Gladys said, "but I knew it was something I had to do on my own. And Mom and Dad didn't freak out—they're actually being supportive. Can you believe it?"

Aunt Lydia took a thoughtful bite of a bright yellow macaron, chewed, and swallowed. "What I can believe," she said finally, "is that you figured out how to deal with this situation all on your own. I'm very impressed, my Gladiola—as usual. But if you tell your editor the truth, she'll likely take back that full-time job offer."

Be honest, Gladys reminded herself. "I've thought about it a lot, and I've decided I'm not ready to go full-time. I'm sorry, Aunt Lydia. I know you were excited about the idea of us working together."

"Oh, don't worry about me," Aunt Lydia said quickly. "Thanks to my work for Mr. Eng, I have more experience now—even if he lets me go, I bet I can find some other kind of job in the food industry. But, Gladys," she continued, placing a hand on her niece's arm, "doesn't this mean you'll have to stop reviewing? You heard Fiona—she won't have a budget left for freelancers in the new year."

"She did say that," Gladys said, "and I understand that's a risk I'll have to take. But I do have one more idea to pitch to her . . . well, if she doesn't have security drag me from the building when she finds out how old I really am."

Aunt Lydia smiled. "Drag you out? Never. If she has any sense at all, she'll find a way to keep you on board. And if she doesn't . . . well, more time for us to cook and practice French together at home! Win-win, *n'est-ce pas?*"

Gladys nodded. She had worried about what Aunt Lydia's reaction would be, but her aunt had pleasantly surprised her almost as much as her parents had. "Thanks, Aunt Lydia," she said. "I couldn't have done any of this without you."

"And without you, my dear, I would probably still be on that couch in that awful T-shirt." Aunt Lydia laughed. "Like I've said before, we make a good team."

Her aunt slipped an arm around Gladys's shoulder and pulled her close, and Gladys hugged her right back. Her whole family was in her corner now; she was ready to take the next step.

Chapter 26

SOMETHING SPECIAL, OFF MENU

FIONA INGLETHORPE STOOD, ONCE AGAIN, in the lobby of the *New York Standard* building, waiting for Gladys Gatsby. She had made another reservation in the *Standard*'s executive dining room, though this time it was only for two people. She supposed that Gladys's daughter was at school today, dressed up in a costume and munching on cheap candy like all the other children. Fiona shuddered. She enjoyed an occasional square of sea-salt-dusted dark chocolate, or a nice artisan truffle, but supersweet American confections generally left her cold.

"Ms. Inglethorpe?"

Fiona spun around, then had to look down to address the speaker. "Coraline?" It seemed that the girl was not off gobbling candy at school after all. "Your—your mother didn't tell me you were coming today." Fiona looked around. "Where *is* your mother, by the way?"

"My mother's not here," the girl said. "My dad came with me, but he has a business meeting, so he'll pick me up in an hour." She turned and waved through the building's glass doors, and a man with glasses and a beaky nose waved back before taking off down the street.

"Wait!" Fiona cried—but it was too late, the man was gone. She turned to the girl, trying to stay calm. "I don't know what's going on here, dear, but I'm a busy woman and I really don't have time to babysit."

"You don't have to babysit anyone," the girl said, "and I'll explain everything over lunch, I promise."

"I'm sorry, Coraline," Fiona replied, "but unless I can speak to Gladys, I really don't think—"

"But that's the thing," the girl said, lowering her voice. "My name's not Coraline. *I'm* Gladys Gatsby."

With a claim like that hanging in the air between them, Fiona had no choice but to usher the girl upstairs.

The elevator ride up to the forty-ninth floor had to be the longest one of Gladys's life. Fiona stared at her with a mixture of confusion, anger, and disappointment on her face, but didn't say a word—probably because there were several other people in the small space with them.

Gladys took advantage of the painful silence to review her proposal for Fiona once more. She had spent a lot of time in the Rabbit Room the previous weekend hammering out the details with Sandy (who had finally wrapped his head around the fact that Gladys had told her parents the truth and the world hadn't ended). They had both agreed that breaking the news to Fiona, though—and proposing a plan by which Gladys could still keep her job with the *New York Standard*—would be trickier.

Finally, Gladys and her editor reached the dining room and were shown to their table.

"Would you like to begin with a drink or an appetizer?" the waiter asked.

"We need some time," Fiona said. "Thank you."

The waiter retreated, and Fiona leaned across the table until her face was dangerously close to Gladys's.

"All right, young lady," she said. "You've got five minutes to explain yourself."

Gladys exhaled the breath she'd been holding. She and Sandy had anticipated such a challenge, and agreed that Gladys should just start at the beginning. "I guess it all began with last year's statewide sixth-grade essay contest," she said. "I wrote my essay in the form of a letter, explaining why I wanted to become a restaurant critic for the *New York Standard*. It didn't win the prize, but then I got an e-mail from you asking for more samples of my writing. You liked them, and then you assigned me to review Classy Cakes."

"That's preposterous," Fiona said. "The letter I received was an official cover letter, applying for the position of freelance restaurant critic with the *Standard*. Not a student *essay*."

But even as the words were coming out of her mouth, Fiona remembered that something had seemed odd about that letter. First of all, it had been printed on pink stationery. And second, it had showed up in her inbox almost immediately after she'd notified Human Resources that she wanted to post an opening for a new critic. She'd always assumed they had already had this letter on file and forwarded it to her right away. Could she have been wrong about that?

But even if HR had not procured her the original application, they had to have gotten involved further down the line. "All my freelancers have to fill out a form for Human Resources with their personal information on it—full name, social security number, etc.—in order to get paid," she said, staring Gladys down.

"I did fill out the forms," Gladys said, remembering the long hunt she and Sandy had undertaken to find her social security card. "And I've been getting the checks; I've just torn them up rather than deposit them, which is why you've been getting those notices from Payroll."

Fiona frowned. "And who, then—if you are, as you claim, Gladys Gatsby—was the woman who came in here with you last time? Are you going to tell me that *that* is Coraline?"

"No, Coraline is a character from a children's book," Gladys said. "That was my aunt Lydia. She was trying to help me keep my cover—you know, like a good restaurant critic does." Gladys hoped she might earn a couple of brownie points with this line, but Fiona still looked livid. "I know that we deceived you, though," Gladys added quickly, "and I'm sorry about that."

Fiona shook her head. "This is quite the story you're telling," she said, "and I'm afraid I'll need a little more proof than just the word of a young girl."

It was time for the next step of Gladys's plan. "I thought you might say that," she said, and she reached into her lobster backpack. "This is my aunt's passport, which she let me borrow for today so you could see her picture and real name. I don't have a picture ID, but here's a copy of my birth certificate, which does have my real name and age on it. And here are my last two reviewing journals, with notes from all the restaurants you assigned me to visit." Gladys placed the books and papers in front of her editor. "And on top of that, my dad said he'd be happy to come up and vouch for me if you want him to. Plus, he's got a bunch of pictures on his phone of us eating hot dogs together for the review I wrote over the summer."

Fiona opened the passport and stared at Lydia's picture, then lifted the birth certificate to examine it more closely. Finally, she thumbed through Gladys's journals before sliding the stack of documents back across the table.

"Passports can be faked," she said coolly. "Birth certificates and journals can be forged. And adults can be persuaded to lie—just as you claim your 'aunt' did the last time you met me."

Gladys opened her mouth to respond, but Fiona held up a pink-nailed finger to stop her.

"I'm a journalist," she said, "and I have training in sniffing out fishy stories. I'm not entirely convinced by your 'evidence,' but I can think of a test that would prove your identity to me."

Here was a development that Gladys and Sandy had *not* anticipated—but she knew that her only option was to agree. "Okay," she said a little breathlessly. "I'll take the test. What is it?"

Fiona pulled a notebook and pen from her own purse. She tore out a sheet of paper and, shielding it from Gladys's eyes with one hand, scribbled something down with the other. She then folded the note in half and called the waiter over. "My apologies," she said, "but I'm going to need Chef Soloway to whip me up something special today, off menu. Please tell him it's for Fiona—he'll understand."

"Yes, ma'am," the waiter said.

"When you bring it to the table, please do so in complete silence," she added. "I do not want the name of this dish or any of its components mentioned."

"Of course," the waiter said, nodding, and he whisked the paper back to the kitchen.

Now Fiona slid the notebook and pen across the table to Gladys. She smiled for the first time, though it did not look very friendly. "Your test," she said quietly, "will be to write a review of our lunch today. I may not know what she looks like, but I know my star reviewer's writing when I read it."

A wave of nervousness coursed through Gladys's body, but it retreated just as quickly as it had arrived. She knew food. She'd read scores of cookbooks from all over the world and cooked hundreds of meals at home.

She steeled herself. She could ace this test. She *would* ace this test. She would prove her identity—and, at the same time, prove to her doubting editor that kids could appreciate more than just chicken fingers and ketchup.

She looked Fiona right in the eye. "I'm ready," she said.

Chapter 27

A BIT OF A PICKLE

If brightly colored pasta—with vegetable-hued shades of orange and green mixed in with the traditional white—is considered kid food, then black pasta is decidedly adult fare. Dyed with squid ink, the linguine I was served at the New York Standard's executive dining room delivered a hint of the sea in every bite. In fact, it almost seemed like it had blown in from the ocean itself, arriving on my plate in a twisted, upside-down tornado that had picked up bits of plump sun-dried tomato and lightly sautéed arugula on its way . . .

GLADYS WROTE AND WROTE. SHE DESCRIBED
the two large scallops—sea scallops, not

bay—that appeared on her plate beside the linguine tornado, their pearly whiteness contrasting elegantly with the pasta's black color. She described the slice of toasted sourdough bread that accompanied her lunch, rubbed with olive oil and garlic and enlivened with a sprinkle of caraway seeds. She even touched on the hint of fresh cucumber flavor in her glass of ice water.

When she finally ran out of things to describe, she paused, reached under the table for her lobster, and unzipped the claw pocket. She had written the review using Fiona's pen, but she wanted to finish it with her own. Uncapping the pen Ms. Quincy had given her, Gladys signed her full name to the bottom of her review in bright green ink. Then she passed the notebook back across the table to her editor.

Fiona reached into her blazer pocket, pulled out a pair of pink reading glasses, and began to examine Gladys's words.

Gladys sat back, relaxing as much as the hard bones of her chair would allow, and watched her editor's expression change. It went from sour to neutral, then from neutral to almost sweet. Fiona even chuckled once. But when she reached the end of the review and looked up, Gladys was surprised to see that she looked furious all over again.

"What's the matter?" Gladys asked. "Didn't I do a good job?"

"You did an outstanding job," Fiona muttered, pulling off her glasses, "which is *exactly* the problem." She dropped her head into her hands and let out a low moan. "Holy basil, I hired a twelve-year-old!"

"Actually, I was eleven when you hired me," Gladys said. "I turned twelve in June."

Fiona's head popped up, her expression now even more stricken. Maybe that had been the wrong thing to say.

"Gadfly tried *so* hard to make me look incompetent this past summer," Fiona continued. "And to think, the evidence was there all along! This is the end of my editing career for sure."

The bubbly, ginger-ale sensation in Gladys's stomach from hearing the word *outstanding* began to fizzle. Her age was going to cost her editor her job? "No!" she cried without thinking, and diners at several tables around them glanced in her direction. *Fudge.* "I mean"—she lowered her voice—"this can't be the end of your career. Not after you pulled out all the stops at the Kids Rock Awards."

"How do you know about that?" Fiona asked.

"I was there," Gladys said. "I came along with my . . . um, friend Hamilton Herbertson. Anyway, I'm the one who sent you that note about how Gilbert Gadfly and Rory Graham were conspiring against you."

"And how did you find *that* out?" Fiona asked.

Gladys shrugged. "I'm a kid. People don't really pay attention to me most of the time. They don't suspect I might be listening in on their private conversations—or that I might be there to review their restaurant. I just blend into the background."

Fiona gave her an appraising look then, as though Gladys was an expensive cut of meat she was considering buying. "Let's go to my office," she said finally.

Five minutes later, they were in Fiona's office on the fourteenth floor, the door shut tight behind them.

"We seem to be in a bit of a pickle," the editor said, sitting down behind her desk. "On one hand, we have a talented restaurant critic who, because of her age, has a very low chance of being recognized by the establishments she is sent to review." Fiona tapped a pink pen against her desktop. "But on the other hand, we have a twelve-year-old child who, if her identity *were* to be discovered, would make this newspaper—and me—the laughingstock of the New York culinary scene.

"Now, first things first," she continued. "That offer I made of permanent employment here is obviously rescinded. Even if I wanted to take you on, it's not legal to hire a twelve-year-old full-time."

Gladys nodded. She had expected this.

"Well, Natalia Bernstein will thank you for her promotion to head critic, anyway," Fiona said. "But the question remains of what to do with you. As I said at our last meeting, my budget for freelancers dries up on January first. And even if I could keep you on in your current role, I'm not sure it would be ethical to do so."

Gladys cleared her throat—the time had finally come to make her proposal. "I have an idea," she said.

Fiona raised an eyebrow. "Go on."

"I love reviewing restaurants for the *Standard*," Gladys said, "but I'm also busy with school. So I was thinking that maybe I could take on fewer assignments—maybe one every couple of months or so. And . . ."—this was the kicker—"maybe I could be honest about my age in the reviews, and gear them more toward younger readers."

Fiona stared at her. "Be *honest*? About your *age*?"

"Yes," Gladys said. "I think kids these days are ready to challenge their palates with more than just chicken fingers. For example, I've been making some unusual sweets for my middle-school bake sales this year—like Indian barfi and Cuban buñuelos—and everyone has loved them. Plus, a lot more people are shopping for international ingredients at my local gourmet grocery, including kids. And I do *not* live in a very adventurous town." Gladys paused for breath; so far, Fiona's expression was inscrutable. "I mean, I'd still do my best to keep my identity a secret from the places I was reviewing, but I could come at a restaurant's menu from a kid's perspective and focus my reviews on what kids might like to eat there. If we got kids to read my reviews, it might persuade them to eat more courageously. *And* it might get restaurants to expand their ideas about what kids are willing to try."

Fiona continued to tap the pen against her desk as she digested Gladys's proposal. "You're passionate about this, aren't you?" she asked finally.

"I'm passionate about good food and good writing," Gladys said.

"And the people who own this newspaper are passionate about expanding our readership," Fiona said. "Launching a new feature that aims to hook new readers when they're young . . . the higher-ups just might go for that."

She gave Gladys her meat-market look again. "Well, Gladys Gatsby, it seems that I owe you an apology. Possibly a whole series of apologies. I've never thought much of children and their culinary capabilities . . . but if there are more kids like you out there, then I've shortchanged quite a chunk of the population with my narrow thinking."

Gladys smiled. If she could get someone as squeamish about kids as Fiona thinking twice, then maybe her new review series really could make a difference.

Fiona stood. "I'll take this up with the paper's publishers, but assuming they approve, then you've got yourself a new gig, Gladys."

Gladys leapt to her feet. "Thank you, Ms. Inglethorpe. And I'm sorry again for all the drama."

The editor waved a hand in the air. "We've been working together long enough now—please call me Fiona." She smiled then, a much warmer smile than the one she'd given Gladys earlier. "But before you go, we have one last item of business to take care of."

"What's that?" Gladys asked.

"The question of your compensation," Fiona said. "Once we bring you on legitimately as a twelve-year-old special correspondent, you'll be able to fill out fresh paperwork for HR—this time, including your birth date. I imagine that you and your parents will need to apply for some sort of special working papers as well, to make sure it's all legal."

"Sure," Gladys said.

"But in the meantime," Fiona continued, "there's the question of your back pay. Is it really true that you've torn up all the checks the *Standard* has sent you?"

"Well, the first one got confiscated by my dad," Gladys said. "Though he thought it was just a mistake, and that the *Standard* meant to send him a tax payment instead. He works for the IRS, and came here in the spring for some meetings," she explained. "The others I did rip up, because, well . . . I didn't think it'd be a good idea for there to be a paper trail since no one here knew how old I really was."

Fiona nodded. "You were covering your tracks. Perhaps not the most mature way to go about it, but I suppose that, given your age, it's understandable. But we can't have you doing all that work for us for free." She opened her desk drawer and pulled out a small booklet. "I'm writing you a new check, with the funds coming straight out of my department's discretionary fund. And this time, you'd better deposit it." She wrote a number on the check in front of her, scribbled her signature, then ripped it from the book and held it out toward Gladys.

"Ms. Inglethorpe—I mean, Fiona—" Gladys stammered. "I can't take this check from you. I've never been in this for the money."

"Business lesson number one," Fiona said, a bit of the old snap returning to her voice. "Never turn down payment for your work." She held the check out across the desk. "Come on now, Gladys—my time is precious, and so is yours, so let's not waste any more of it."

At a loss for what else to do, Gladys slipped the check into her lobster backpack.

"Well, it's been an . . . enlightening day, Gladys," Fiona said. "I look forward to learning more from you as this project progresses."

She held her right hand out, and Gladys—who had to angle her own right arm upward to reach—shook hands with her editor.

"Thank you so much for this opportunity," she said. "Oh, and Happy Halloween."

Chapter 28

TOO MUCH CANDY CORN

GLADYS WAS STILL ON CLOUD NINE when she stepped off the train that evening with her dad. She had spent the afternoon back at his office in downtown Manhattan, and he had responded enthusiastically to her good job news—though he was even more excited when Gladys showed him the check Fiona had written to her.

"Six thousand dollars?!" he shrieked.

"Yep," Gladys said. "A thousand for each review."

"Well, interest rates aren't very high these days," he said, "but still, that'll be a nice nest egg for your college fund." He offered to hold the check in his own wallet for safekeeping, and Gladys had agreed. She'd also logged on to DumpMail from her dad's work computer to send Sandy a message, letting him know how the meeting had gone. Although she would have rather told him in person, she knew that there wouldn't be time tonight since she was heading straight to the Halloween dance.

Charissa had invited Gladys, Parm, Rolanda, and Marti over to get ready for the dance together. The train Gladys and her dad were on arrived at East Dumpsford Station at 5:55, and the dance started at 6:30, so she didn't have much time. Luckily, her mom was waiting to pick them up, and her costume was already in the trunk.

Her mom had to drive more slowly than usual because of the kids trick-or-treating in the last of East Dumpsford's daylight, and with every second that passed, Gladys's nervousness about the dance mounted. She wished that Aunt Lydia had been there to help distract her, but her aunt was holding down the fort at the Gatsbys' house, giving out packets of plump dried pears that Mr. Eng's was now carrying on her recommendation.

"Have a great time!" Gladys's mom called as Gladys sprinted up Charissa's long driveway. Just as her parents were about to pull away, another car pulled up behind them. Parm jumped out, dressed in her soccer uniform and carrying her backpack, and raced up the driveway behind Gladys.

"Hey!" Gladys greeted her. "I was sure I'd be the last one here."

"We had an away game in Oceanside," Parm gasped, almost breathless. "Just got back."

Up in Charissa's room, a Sasha McRay album was blaring and Rolanda and Marti were already in their matching black witch costumes accented with sparkling sequins. Charissa, still in her fluffy mauve bathrobe, was braiding Marti's thick red hair, and Rolanda was perched in front of Charissa's three-way mirror, applying makeup.

"Hey, girls!" Charissa snapped an elastic band in place around the base of Marti's braid. "Welcome to Dance Prep Central. Omigosh, I can't wait to see your costumes!"

Gladys was also eager to get a look at her costume, since her aunt had made some alterations to it while she was in the city. She tossed her bag onto Charissa's canopy bed and unzipped it, exposing bright orange fabric with black accents.

"You're dressing as a pumpkin?" Marti asked incredulously.

Rolanda looked up from her makeup. "Isn't that, like, a little kid's costume?"

Gladys had never liked those two much.

"It's not just a pumpkin," she said. She pulled the costume free from its bag. Sewn onto the front, instead of the triangles of a jack-o'-lantern's eyes and nose, was a symbol she had learned all about at the Mathletes bake sale: π.

"I'm going as pumpkin pi," she explained.

Marti stared. "I don't get it."

"It's a math joke," Rolanda said. "Or . . . a food joke?"

"It's both," Charissa declared, "and I *love* it." The other girls shrugged and went back to primping. "Parm, did you want to shower before you changed? There's a towel on that shelf."

"No thanks," Parm said, tossing her backpack onto the floor. "And anyway, I'm not changing."

"Did you forget your costume?" Charissa asked.

"Nope," Parm said. "I'm just not into dressing up. I think it's dumb." She glanced quickly around the room. "No offense."

Charissa looked horrified. "Parm, you've *got* to have a costume! It's Halloween!" She crossed the room and snatched her own witch outfit off its hanger on the closet door. "Here, wear mine," she said.

"What? No way." Parm shot Gladys a frantic look. "Gladys, back me up here."

Gladys, who was in the process of pulling on a pair of green tights, feared that her friend had entered into a losing battle. "I dunno, Parm," she said in a playful tone. "You may not have a choice. I once heard a very wise man say, 'Whatever Charissa wants, Charissa gets.'"

"That's right!" Charissa cried. "And all I want for Halloween is for Parm to dress up and look beautiful

and have a great time at the dance. Come on—put that on, and I'll do your hair, too."

"Charissa!" Marti whined. "You can't give her your costume. We're supposed to be the three witches from MacBook!"

"Macbeth," Rolanda corrected her. "The three witches from *Macbeth*. It's only one of *Shakespeare's* most famous plays!" She shook her head, braids swinging—but Gladys had to wonder whether Rolanda had been so knowledgeable about Shakespeare before she'd joined the Drama Club.

"There will still be three witches," Charissa told Marti. "You, Rolanda, and Parm."

"And what will you be?" Marti asked.

Charissa gazed around the room until her eyes rested on Parm again. "I'll be a soccer player," she declared. "Parm, we'll switch. You'll wear my costume, and I'll wear your uniform."

"My uniform's not a costume," Parm said.

"Sure it is," Charissa countered. "At least, for me it is. It's something I wouldn't wear unless I was dressing up as another person. And the whole point of wearing a costume is to feel what it's like to be in someone else's shoes, right?" She glanced down at Parm's muddy soccer cleats. "You'll need to lend me your shoes, too."

"This is crazy," Parm said. "*You're* crazy."

"Yeah, but you love me anyway." Charissa grinned. "Now come on, get changed."

"I can't believe I'm doing this," Parm grumbled, but just the same, she kicked off her cleats and began to change her clothes. Luckily, she had some fresh socks and shin guards in her bag so Charissa didn't have to use her dirty ones.

Twenty minutes later, they all piled into Charissa's mother's SUV. Parm's eyes glittered with sparkly purple shadow, and her long hair was swept up into an elegant swirl. Charissa, meanwhile, had commandeered Parm's stretchy headband and two of her black under-eye stickers, as well as her uniform, and looked like a fierce soccer warrior.

Gladys tugged on the hem of her orange outfit and wondered if it was possible for a pumpkin to be filled with butterflies.

The sun was down by the time they reached the school, but light and loud music spilled out from the open gym doors. The girls tumbled out of the car and joined the stream of seventh- and eighth-graders making their way toward the entrance.

"Hey, it's witches!" a boy's voice called out. "Real original."

Owen sauntered up to their group, flanked by two other boys Gladys knew from elementary school: Jake Wheeler and Ethan Slezak. Jake wore a furry tunic and Viking helmet, and Ethan was dressed as some sort of robot. Owen, though, was dressed simply in jeans and a black hoodie.

"We're not *just* witches," Rolanda said sniffily. "We're the *three* witches from *Macbeth*."

"Yeah!" Marti chimed in. "Bubble, bubble toil and trouble!"

"It's *double, double,* not bubble, bubble," Rolanda hissed, but Owen and his entourage were already howling with laughter.

"You're one to laugh," Parm snapped at Owen, "considering you didn't even bother to wear a costume!"

Owen stopped laughing and beckoned Jake and Ethan to move off with him. "Hey, save me a slow dance, will ya, Parm?" he called over his shoulder.

"Not on your life," Parm muttered.

Charissa slung an arm around Parm's shoulders. "I knew you'd see the light about costumes," she said. "Come on—let's get inside. Gladys has to meet up with her hot date."

"Not a date!" Gladys reminded her, but she fell into step with the other girls anyway.

Giant pumpkins, fuzzy fake cobwebs, and orange-and-black streamers decorated the gym, and one side of the room was flanked with long tables holding cups of punch and bowls of chips and candy. A few kids were already dancing, but a lot more were milling around the refreshment tables or clustered by the doorway. Charissa had to push through them to clear a path for her friends.

Meanwhile, Gladys—whose heart was thumping now

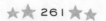

in time to the bass pouring from the DJ's speakers—looked everywhere for Hamilton. They should have set a specific spot to meet. There were hundreds of kids here, almost all in costume. How was she supposed to pick him out?

"Gladys?"

She glanced up—and had to suppress a scream. Standing before her was a boy who looked like he'd been shot in the head and had half the flesh on his face eaten off by maggots.

But he was also wearing a beret.

"Hamilton?" she squeaked. "Oh my *goodness*! You're a . . ."

"Zombie," he answered. "Specifically, Mr. Masterson, father of Grady, protagonist of *Zombietown, U.S.A.* What do you think?"

"Extremely. Terrifying," Gladys told him truthfully. Hamilton grinned, and she was glad to see he at least hadn't gone as far as getting a set of fake bloody teeth.

"My mother knows a Broadway makeup artist," he said. "She came over to help me get ready."

"Wow—you took this really seriously," Gladys said. "I got dressed in about five minutes."

"And you look great!" Hamilton said quickly. "Pumpkin pi—really clever."

"Thanks."

They stood there awkwardly then, looking around. Gladys's friends had moved to the refreshment table,

and now she felt a sudden hankering for candy corn.

"Come on," she said. "Let's get something to eat. Charissa's here, and I'll introduce you to Parm."

Over the next hour, more students arrived at the gym, and the trickle of dancers out on the floor turned into a raging river of kids showing off their moves. Gladys wasn't big on dancing, but Hamilton insisted that they join the party. "After all, this may be the only school dance of my entire life!" he said. "It would be foolish not to take advantage."

Gladys was relieved that at least no one was pairing off, so she was able to dance clumsily alongside Hamilton as part of a larger group that also included Charissa, Parm, Rolanda, and Marti. Elaine de la Vega—whose costume consisted of fake glasses and a laminated PRESS badge—moved all around the gym snapping pictures. Gladys also kept catching glimpses of Owen and his buddies skirting the perimeter of their dance circle, but every few minutes Charissa shot Owen a death glare, and they backed away.

Their group was rehydrating with cups of punch (a disgusting "red" flavor, but still, Gladys was thirsty) when the DJ's voice crooned out over the speaker system. "We're gonna slow things down now," she said. "This next dance is for all you couples out there."

Hamilton cleared his throat. "Er, Gladys," he started, "would you have any interest—"

"Yo, Parm!" Owen's voice seemed to carry over the

crowd as he ran toward their group at full tilt. Hamilton was barely able to jump out of the way before Owen's sneakers skidded to a stop right in front of Parm's pointy witch shoes. Breathing heavily, Owen knocked his hood back from his head. "Will you dance with me?"

Parm stared at him for a bewildered moment, then, drawing herself up to her full height, said, "Okay, fine."

Gladys nearly choked on her punch—but that was nothing compared with Charissa's reaction. As Parm and Owen walked together out onto the dance floor, her lower lip trembled in wordless shock. A moment later, when Owen put his hands on Parm's waist, Charissa ripped off her headband, flung it to the ground, and raced toward the door that led to the hallway.

Gladys stared at the couple on the dance floor, then at Charissa's retreating back—which, ironically, said *Singh.* Something was coming together in her head.

"I'm sorry, Hamilton," she said. "I'd better go see if Charissa's okay."

"Of course," Hamilton said. "I'll be right here."

Gladys took off into the hallway and just caught sight of the girls' bathroom door swinging shut behind her friend. She found Charissa standing by the sinks, gazing down into one of them. No one else was in the bathroom.

"Charissa," Gladys said. "I'm sorry."

Charissa turned to her and sniffled. "Am I that obvious?"

"No! I mean, I doubt anyone else noticed anything. And definitely not Owen."

"What do I care if Owen notices?" Charissa said.

Now Gladys was confused. "Wait. Don't you have a crush on him? I thought that was why you were upset."

Charissa stared at her. "*What?* No way! Owen Green . . . I mean . . . he didn't even wear a costume!" She kicked the toe of one of Parm's soccer cleats into the cinder-block bathroom wall. "I'm upset because Parm is dancing with him, and . . . because I like her."

"Well, I'm glad to hear that," Gladys said. "I think it's really great that the two of you have become friends."

"No," Charissa said quietly. Her gray eyes locked onto Gladys's. "I *like* her."

"Oh." Gladys blinked. *"Oh."*

Charissa turned and looked at herself in the mirror. She balled up the front of Parm's soccer jersey in her fist, then let it fall back against her torso. "God, I wish I'd brought a different outfit to change into. I look so stupid."

"Charissa—" Gladys started.

"Let's not make a big deal of this, okay?" Charissa said. "Owen's into Parm, and she's apparently into him. Parm and I are just friends, and that's how it is."

Gladys bit her lip. "Okay," she said. "But if you ever want to talk more . . . well, I'm here."

Charissa tried to smile. "I know."

Gladys stepped forward and gathered her friend into a hug. Charissa sank into her, her body shaking slightly. Gladys squeezed her tighter.

"Don't say anything to her, okay?" Charissa whispered. "I'm not ready for anyone else to know."

"Of course," Gladys said. This was Charissa's business, to share whenever and with whomever she chose.

"Thanks." Charissa stepped back, then pulled out her phone. "I'm gonna text Daddy to come pick me up. I'm not really in the mood for dancing anymore. Do you think you can get a ride home with someone else?"

"Yeah, no problem," Gladys said.

Charissa finished sending her text, then Gladys walked her out to the front exit. They waited together in silence for Charissa's father to come, and when his dark sedan pulled up, Gladys gave Charissa another hug.

"Are you gonna be okay?" Gladys asked.

"Yeah, don't worry about me," Charissa said. "If the others ask, you can tell them I got sick—too much candy corn or something."

"There's no such thing," Gladys said, and they exchanged a smile.

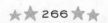

"You're a good friend, Gladys," Charissa said. "And Hamilton's lucky to be your boyfriend."

"He's not—" Gladys started, but Charissa was already dashing toward her dad's car.

Gladys was halfway down the hallway that led back to the gym when a zombie shuffled up to her.

"Gladys!" Hamilton cried. "I was starting to worry."

"Sorry," she said. "Charissa wasn't feeling great, so I waited with her 'til her dad could come take her home."

"Ah." Though it was hard to tell under the makeup, she thought she saw his expression soften. "I thought maybe you'd decided to abandon me here—you know, give me a taste of my own medicine for disappearing on you."

Gladys shook her head. "I'm not that vengeful. And I'm really glad you're back in town."

"I'm glad, too." He smiled. "Well, shall we return to the gymnasium?"

Gladys stepped up close to him, then took his hand into her own. It was warm and slightly moist. He didn't pull it away.

"Yeah," she said. "Let's go."

They made it back to the dance just in time for the last slow song of the night.

Chapter 29

RETURN OF THE BLOWTORCH

"SO, GIRLS, HOW WAS THE BIG DANCE?" Parm's mother asked as Parm and Gladys climbed into her car.

"Fine!" Parm said quickly. "Right, Gladys?"

"Yeah, it was fine," Gladys said. She hadn't actually had much of a chance to talk to Parm other than to ask if she could catch a ride home with her. Parm and Owen had spent the rest of the dance together, which pretty much made them an official DTMS couple—though it didn't sound like Parm was eager to share that news with her mother. Then again, Gladys wasn't exactly planning to blab all the details of her time with Hamilton to her own parents, so she understood.

Mrs. Singh started the engine. "Parminder, what are you wearing?"

"Oh . . . Charissa lent me a costume," Parm said. "And actually, she has my soccer stuff. But I'm sure we can swap back at school."

"The last I heard, you were dead set against dressing up." Mrs. Singh sounded amused. "What's next— will I find you at the refrigerator at midnight, stuffing yourself with my cooking?"

"Geez, Mom—a person can change her mind about one thing, can't she?"

"I believe she can," Mrs. Singh said merrily.

When Gladys arrived home, she found her mother rereading *Zombietown, U.S.A.*—her own copy now finally signed by the author. "Aunt Lydia and Dad went to bed," she told Gladys. "But *I* stayed up to wait for you. What an exciting day you've had! I want to hear all about it."

Gladys told her mom about her meeting with Fiona, her lunch review "test," and the Halloween dance— leaving out certain bits, of course. "But getting back to the *Standard* job," she said. "Fiona gave me a check. A pretty big one."

"Yes, your father showed me," her mom said. "We'll take it to the bank tomorrow and put it straight into your savings account."

"Actually," Gladys said, "I had another idea of what to do with it. Kind of . . . an investment. But I'd need your help to make it happen."

Gladys explained her idea. Her mom was skeptical

at first, but Gladys made her argument convincingly and, in the end, managed to win her mother over.

"There's no guarantee you'll make your money back," her mom warned, "but it sounds like you've thought through the risks."

"I have," Gladys said.

"Then I'll put in the paperwork tomorrow morning," her mom said, "and if all goes well, you can make the announcement at dinner."

The next day at school couldn't go by fast enough. Once again, Gladys found herself wishing she had a phone, if only to text her mom and find out how their plan was coming along.

Okay, and she wouldn't have minded texting Hamilton, either. She wondered if there was any wiggle room in the "no phone 'til you're thirteen" plan; if so, she might be willing to scrap her Christmas wish list in exchange for one.

Between fourth and fifth periods, Gladys spotted Charissa and Parm leaving their math classroom together. Their usual roles were reversed: Parm was chattering happily while Charissa listened, her expression rather blank. As she passed them, Gladys caught a wisp of their conversation. "And then he said, 'Ya wanna get some ice cream on Saturday?' And, well, I don't *like* ice cream, but I said okay anyway, so . . ."

Gladys's heart gave a pang for Charissa as her two friends were swallowed up in the crowd.

At the end of French class, Madame Goldstein reminded them that the French Club would meet after school as usual the following Tuesday. "And those of you who are members, please bring some ideas for our bake sale fund-raiser in two weeks!"

Gladys groaned inwardly—after soccer, Drama Club, Mathletes, and Chess Club, she had hoped to be done with bake sales for a while. But she supposed that, for the one club she actually *wanted* to be a member of, she could make an exception. With her green pen, she made a note on her hand to ask her aunt if she had any tips for making macarons at home.

That night, after a Gladys-cooked dinner of butternut squash soup and fresh corn bread, her mom stood up. "I believe that Gladys has some important documents to share," she said with a smile, pulling some papers out of her briefcase.

Gladys took the pages from her mother. "It's a lease on the old Pathetti's Pies building," she announced.

Aunt Lydia laughed. "On top of everything else, are you opening a restaurant?"

Gladys shook her head, then passed the papers over to her aunt. "No, Aunt Lydia. *You're* opening a restaurant."

Aunt Lydia blinked at her. *"Excusez-moi?"*

★★ 271 ★★

Gladys's dad—who had been updated on the plan by her mom—jumped in. "Gladys has chosen to invest her *Standard* earnings in a local small business," he said. "Instead of sticking them in the bank, she's used them to lease the building. Jen and I thought it sounded like such a good idea that we've thrown in some of our own funds as well. Gladys requested that the lease be in your name, Lydia, and that you be given full control of the menu and décor—though she'll be available to consult on these things if her opinion is needed."

"It really worked out perfectly," Gladys's mom added. "The building's owner doesn't want to pay for a renovation, but Gladys said you would want to decorate the café yourself anyway. In exchange—and because, to be honest, he had no other offers—I was able to negotiate a nice discount on the rent. For our combined investment, the place is yours for six months."

Aunt Lydia's mouth opened and closed like she was a fish that had just been yanked out of the water.

"I know it's not Paris," Gladys said, "but this town's tastes are changing. I can tell just by how busy Mr. Eng's is now! People are cooking more, and have higher expectations of their meals. I think the time is finally right for East Dumpsford to have a decent restaurant—don't you?"

Aunt Lydia still seemed unable to speak.

"And once my new column for the *Standard* starts

up," Gladys said, "hopefully even more kids around here will be interested in eating adventurously. In fact, the French Club at school is raising money for a field trip to a French restaurant. Usually they go into the city, but if your place is up and running, I bet I could get them to keep the trip here this year. Less money spent on transportation means more for cassoulet and vichyssoise, right?"

Tears streamed down Aunt Lydia's cheeks. "I don't deserve you," she blubbered. "I don't deserve any of you!"

The Gatsbys piled in on Lydia with hugs, words of encouragement, and fresh napkins into which she could blow her nose. Finally, she pulled herself together.

"I'll pay back every penny," she promised them. "With interest—a magnificent amount of interest. Even if this project fails, I will find a way."

"We believe in you, Aunt Lydia," Gladys said. "I know things were rough at your old job, and at Mr. Eng's at the beginning, but you really thrived when he sent you out to those trade shows. You know good food, and you know how to follow your vision. You'll be great at launching your own restaurant."

A fresh set of tears was welling up in her aunt's eyes, though she smiled through them. "Your faith in me means so much, my sweet star."

"Ditto," Gladys said. "Now, let's start planning! Mom, do you have the keys yet? We can go in and start repainting this weekend! Dad, can we borrow some of your power tools?"

"We'll see . . ." he replied, giving Gladys a long look. "We all know what happened the last time you got your hands on a blowtorch."

Chapter 30

THE CAFÉ DE PARIS

*The Dumpsford Township
Middle School* Telegraph
—January 14 issue

FRENCH CLUB MEMBERS EXPAND THEIR PALATES AT NEWLY OPENED RESTAURANT

A Special Report by Gladys Gatsby

Opened to the public only last week, Café de Paris is in the old Pathetti's Pies building, though you would never know that from looking at it. Repainted a cheerful eggshell blue and sporting wrought-iron chairs and tables, the restaurant has instantly become the most chic dining spot our town has to offer.

DTMS's French Club took a trip there last week.

A New York native, owner Lydia Winslow has spent the last decade living in Paris, where she managed a small café in the Montmartre neighborhood. While the French Club students enjoyed an *amuse-bouche* (literally translated as "mouth amuser"—in other words, a small, complimentary appetizer), Ms. Winslow regaled them with tales of her years in France, peppering her speech with French phrases, much to the delight of club adviser and French teacher Lillian Goldstein.

The four-course menu featured something for every palate, beginning with an enticingly flavored cold vichyssoise (potato soup). The club's outing was funded by the proceeds from their November bake sale, which introduced middle-school students to macarons and madeleines, two delicate French confections. It also raised the club's profile at the school and increased membership by 50 percent.

One of the newest members is Hamilton Herbertson, who is actually homeschooled because of his busy career as a best-selling author. "I recently learned that homeschooled students in East Dumpsford are permitted to participate in public school extracurricular activities!" he told the *Telegraph* excitedly. "So I signed up for French Club right away. I toured in France, you know, so I picked up a bit of the language." When asked how the Café de Paris stacked up to some of the French restaurants he ate at during his tour, he said, "Oh, this café can stand with any of them. In fact, I'd say it's superior to most—and much more romantic."

Another new French Club member is Elaine de la Vega, editor in chief of the *Telegraph*. "It's nice to enjoy a night off from reporting," she said, slurping her soup, "especially now that I have trustworthy staffers covering news for the paper."

The French Club members were not the only patrons visiting the café on the night in question. While they dug into their main course of cassoulet (a stew from the southern region of France consisting of white beans and various flavorful meats), a mother and son sitting at a smaller table by the door were finishing their dinner with a cheese plate.

"It's been just lovely," local resident Jayne Anderson replied when asked about her experience dining at the café. "Every course cooked to perfection." Her son, eleven-year-old Sandy, seemed to agree. Although his mouth was full of cheese when asked what he thought of the food, he uttered the word *odoriferous!* with gusto. He was later observed asking Ms. Winslow for a doggy bag of her stinkiest chèvre to take with him into school the next day.

Other patrons that night included Robert Eng, owner of Mr. Eng's Gourmet Grocery. "I supply the produce for this restaurant," he told the *Telegraph* proudly. "Ms. Winslow is a former employee of mine, and I'm happy to see her running her own establishment—and making such nice use of my shop's gourmet ingredients." He was enjoying a frisée salad with a delicate poached egg on top.

When surveyed, all but one of the French Club members said that they would be happy to return to the restaurant and try more dishes. The only holdout was Parminder Singh, who did not touch a bite, despite the coaching of her friend Charissa Bentley. When asked whether she thought her tastes might change in the future, she shrugged.

It's been a long journey for Ms. Winslow, but she told the *Telegraph* that she's "happy to be home at last." And East Dumpsford is *très heureux* (that is, very happy) to have her.

To see Café de Paris's hours and find a coupon for a 20 percent student discount, please turn to the restaurant's full-color ad on page 3.

ACKNOWLEDGMENTS

WRITING GLADYS GATSBY'S STORY HAS been an incredibly sweet undertaking for me, and once again I'm happy to acknowledge the many people who made this series possible.

Huge thanks to my editor, Shauna Rossano, for her endless enthusiasm for Gladys's continuing adventures. Striving to write to her high standards has made these books immeasurably better. Kelly Murphy has once again elevated Gladys's story with her beautiful cover art. Thank you also to Susan Kochan, Katherine Perkins, Amanda Mustafic, and the entire team at Penguin Young Readers for everything you do to get these books out into the world and into the hands of kids and kids at heart. And thank you to my agent, Ammi-Joan Paquette, who has believed in Gladys since day one.

Jessica Lawson, Rebecca Behrens, and Lauren Sabel—I'm so grateful for your speedy beta reads and generous feedback on early drafts of this book. *Stars So Sweet* will be in exalted company on the shelves beside your 2016 novels! And thank you to the Paul sisters for your feedback and encouragement at crucial moments.

I'm indebted to the many friends on Facebook and Twitter (and the couple I randomly accosted at a coffee shop in Denver) who gamely quizzed their kids and reached back to their own childhoods to respond to my crowdsourcing queries about middle-school life.

I wrote and revised much of this book as I traveled and held events to promote *The Stars of Summer*, and I could not have managed that schedule without a lot of help from family and friends. Andy Cahill, Barbara and Fred Dairman, Judy Gruber, Brooke Dairman and Aaron Hollon, Heidi and Matt Cahill, and Katie Wade, thank you for the cooking, chauffeuring, guest beds, your (sometimes forcible) recruiting of event attendees . . . and most importantly, your love and support.

Finally, to the readers, teachers, librarians, booksellers, and book club leaders who have championed the All Four Stars series, thank you for accepting Gladys and her friends into your hearts.